Jane Eyre

Charlotte Brontë

A Samuel French Acting Edition

SAMUELFRENCH-LONDON.CO.UK
SAMUELFRENCH.COM

Copyright © 1996 by Charles Vance
All Rights Reserved

JANE EYRE is fully protected under the copyright laws of the British Commonwealth, including Canada, the United States of America, and all other countries of the Copyright Union. All rights, including professional and amateur stage productions, recitation, lecturing, public reading, motion picture, radio broadcasting, television and the rights of translation into foreign languages are strictly reserved.

ISBN 978-0-573-01803-9

www.samuelfrench-london.co.uk

www.samuelfrench.com

FOR AMATEUR PRODUCTION ENQUIRIES

UNITED KINGDOM AND WORLD EXCLUDING NORTH AMERICA

plays@SamuelFrench-London.co.uk

020 7255 4302/01

Each title is subject to availability from Samuel French, depending upon country of performance.

CAUTION: Professional and amateur producers are hereby warned that *JANE EYRE* is subject to a licensing fee. Publication of this play does not imply availability for performance. Both amateurs and professionals considering a production are strongly advised to apply to the appropriate agent before starting rehearsals, advertising, or booking a theatre. A licensing fee must be paid whether the title is presented for charity or gain and whether or not admission is charged.

The professional rights in this play are controlled by Samuel French Ltd, 52 Fitzroy Street, London, W1T 5JR.

No one shall make any changes in this title for the purpose of production. No part of this book may be reproduced, stored in a retrieval system, or transmitted in any form, by any means, now known or yet to be invented, including mechanical, electronic, photocopying, recording, videotaping, or otherwise, without the prior written permission of the publisher. No one shall upload this title, or part of this title, to any social media websites.

The right of Charlotte Brontë to be identified as author of this work has been asserted by her in accordance with Section 77 of the Copyright, Designs and Patents Act 1988

JANE EYRE

First presented at the Forum Theatre, Billingham, on 20th February, 1996 with the following cast of characters:

Adèle Varens	Lucy Morgans
Leah, a housemaid	Verona Chard
Mrs Fairfax	Barbara Murray
Grace Poole	Maggie Stables
Jane Eyre	Jill Greenacre
John, a footman	James Campbell
Edward Rochester	George Chakiris
Blanche Ingram	Marianna Reidman
Richard Mason	Nicholas Briggs
Reverend Wood	Dennis Spencer
Bertha	Marianna Reidman

Directed by Charles Vance
Designed by Robert Sherwood
Lighting by Bob Bustance

CHARACTERS

Adèle Varens
Leah, a housemaid
Mrs Fairfax
Grace Poole
Jane Eyre
John, a footman
Edward Rochester
Blanche Ingram
Richard Mason
Reverend Wood
Bertha

SYNOPSIS OF SCENES

ACT I
  SCENE 1 October 1846
  SCENE 2 January 1847
  SCENE 3 Five hours later
  SCENE 4 April 1847
  SCENE 5 Several hours later

ACT II
  SCENE 1 July 1847
  SCENE 2 March 1848
  SCENE 3 Some hours later
  SCENE 4 Four days later

The action takes place in the Library of Thornfield Hall at Milcote, Yorkshire —1846-48

PRODUCTION NOTES

Jane Eyre is one of the most loved classic novels in the English language and to translate it to the theatre presents the adapter with much soul-searching. To embrace the whole of the story of the orphaned child who suffered at the hands of her aunt, Mrs Reed and Brocklehurst, the principal of Lowood School; her arrival at Thornfield to become governess to Rochester's ward, Adèle; her flight after the disclosure of Rochester's dreadful secret; her life with St John Rivers and her new found independence prior to her return to Rochester would, I suspect, take some eight or nine hours of performance, reminiscent of the marathon *Nicholas Nickleby* at the RSC.

I chose to focus on the love story of Jane and Rochester which enabled me to contain the action in a single setting, with the exception of one small inset scene. But it also meant that, instead of going with Jane (in what is a first-person novel) after her flight from her aborted wedding, I have kept the action at Thornfield and told the dramatic story of the fire which blinds Rochester and the return of Jane after she hears Rochester's voice calling to her to reunite the hapless lovers after the death of his wife.

To the purist this could appear to be a form of sacrilege, particularly in those scenes after Jane has flown. I believe this is justified in that I was faithful to those aspects of the story that related to Jane when she received news of the tragedy which struck Thornfield. Certainly audiences throughout a long national tour found it theatrically rewarding and the many students and scholars who saw the production were generous in their appraisal of our loyalty to the original text.

I think that in the minimum possible reportage we manage to convey the essence of those long passages of the novel which have been omitted from the playscript and for those studying the book for examinations or research I prepared "Clue Notes" which deal succinctly with the "before and after" of the story.

Certainly it makes for exciting theatre and its staging provides many opportunities for the imaginative director.

The play is set in Rochester's library which is turned over to Jane as her quarters and school-room and the important wedding scene is stylized by using a single stained glass window in front of which the marriage ceremony is played. This should be within the resources of even the smallest company.

There are eleven characters in the play and I doubled the roles of Blanche Ingram and Bertha Rochester which worked well. Music plays a vital role in the adaptation and does much to establish the dramatically changing moods of the scenes in a play with two acts and nine scenes!

I originally broke the action into three acts as I wanted a "break" from the action after the flight from the church. Subsequently I was persuaded that it made sense to play the script in two acts with an interval after the fifth scene of the play. This presents the actor playing Rochester with a very quick change from wedding clothes back to working costume, but we found that it was worth the effort for the dramatic values it afforded.

I am a committed Brontë devotee and derived great pleasure both from adapting the book (as I did from her sister's novel *Wuthering Heights*) and I found the rehearsal process as a director especially rewarding. I would like to think that I have given any cast approaching my script total artistic freedom.

Charles Vance
Adapter/director

Also by Charles Vance, published by Samuel French

Wuthering Heights
adapted from the novel by Emily Brontë

ACT I

Scene 1

The library of Thornfield Hall at Milcote, Yorkshire. An evening in October 1846

It is an imposing room upon the first floor of this, a large country mansion. There is a large leaded casement window in the R wall which opens out of the set with a built-in window seat. There is an archway UL with a passage to Jane's bedroom. Below this is an imposing fireplace, dominated by a large portrait of Rochester's father. A pair of double doors UC, opens on to the passageway where we can see the beginning of a stairway UC, leading to the rooms on the second floor which house Grace Poole and Bertha, and the entrance to Rochester's room and its interior when the door is open. Recessed bookshelves are either side of the casement window and double doors. (See ground plan and Setting Note on page 66)

The room itself, whilst imposing and indicative of Rochester's substantial means, is relatively sparsely furnished and with little decorative dressing or painting. There are some framed maps on the walls complementing the large globe of the world DL. The central focus is a large winged leather armchair at C (Rochester's own chair) with a period settle LC, in front of which is a long upholstered stool. A medium-sized table, DR below the bookshelves, can be opened in later scenes to become Adèle's work table and there are several upholstered upright chairs in the room. In the original production there was a pedestal with a large bust and the backing behind the double doors was dressed with tapestries rather than paintings

As the CURTAIN *rises it is early evening on a dull October day and we can see Leah, a young pleasant-looking parlour-maid briskly tidying the room. Adèle Varens, a pretty French child of not more than twelve years of age is dancing about the room and singing*

Adèle (*singing*) Elle était un' bergè-re
 Et ron, ron, ron, petit pat-a-pon,
 Elle était un' bergè-re.
 Qui gardait ses moutons, ron, ron,
 Qui gardait ses moutons.

Leah (*taking little notice of Adèle*) Mind out the way, miss...
Adèle Elle fit un fromage,
Et ron, ron, ron, petit pat-a-pon.
Elle fit un fromage...
(*She breaks off*) Leah, Leah, you must look at me — I dance for you — look!
Elle fit un fromage,
Et ron, ron, ron, petit pat-a-pon,
Leah (*over Adèle*) Oh, you funny little thing ...
Adèle Elle fit un fromage,
Du lait de ses moutons, ron, ron,
Du lait de ses moutons ...
Leah (*as she is finishing the last line*) You'll be in trouble if Mrs Fairfax sees you.
Adèle Non, non — she likes me to dance for her — I am dancing for you, Leah — you must see me.
Leah I've got too much to do with the lady arriving.
Adèle But I am pretty at the dancing — at 'ome with Mamma she teaches me — I am clever dancing ——
Leah Dancer — that you may be — I don't know about clever — though.
Adèle Je ne comprends pas — I — I am not clever?
Leah You're very sure of yourself, aren't you?
Adèle Ah — Leah ... (*Running to her and hugging her*) You not love me now?
Leah (*laughing*) Not when you stop me doing my work.
Adèle (*innocently*) I not stop you.
Leah Oh, yes you do.
Adèle (*coyly*) Oh, no — not I — (*She quickly snatches Leah's duster and dances away from her laughing*) I 'elp you — look — I 'elp!
Leah No, Miss Adèle — no — come 'ere with my duster, Miss Adèle.
Adèle I 'elp you. (*Singing*) I 'elp you — I 'elp you!
Leah Oh come, miss, please — I shall catch it if I don't finish things for the new lady — Oh, I shall be in trouble.
Adèle Mais oui — mais oui — pour ma gouvernante — I be good. (*She returns the duster*) When — when she come, Leah?
Leah I don't know.
Adèle Mais oui — you prepare for her.
Leah I know, but I don't know when.
Adèle Ce soir? This night?
Leah Yes, sometime.
Adèle 'Ow long — 'ow long will it be?
Leah I don't know these things.
Adèle Ooh, I am so — so — ooh — qu'est-ce-que-c'est?

Act I, Scene 1

Leah You're looking forward to 'er coming — we all are.
Adèle Mais oui. Je parle si mal Anglais. Je pourrai causer avec elle ...
Leah Oh, now don't start that French talking — I don't understand ...
Adèle Mais oui — mais oui — I teach — I teach — (*Mannered*) Bon soir, Leah. (*Running round the room*) Il-y-a la table — la porte — la fenêtre — la tête — le coeur — le bras — la jambe — écoutez, Leah!
Leah (*laughing*) I don't — I don't understand ——
Adèle Mais non, Leah, tu ne comprends pas. (*She laughs*) Ooh, I am so 'appy ma gouvernante arrive ...
Leah "Governess" — see, I know that.
Adèle Oui, Gov-er-ness — she comes — she teaches me.
Leah We won't be ready for her if I don't hurry.
Adèle I will be happy to see her before the sleep.
Leah Not tonight — not if she's late — Mrs Fairfax will have you in bed.
Adèle Non! Non! I will not go. (*She stamps her foot*) I will not...
Leah You'll have to ...
Adèle Mais non. I will not go to bed. I run away!
Leah (*laughing*) No, you won't.
Adèle I will — I will — I hide — Oui, oui, I hide ...

Adèle runs from the room

Leah is laughing

Mrs Fairfax (*off*) Adèle! Adèle! Where are you going?
Adèle (*off*) Non! Non!
Mrs Fairfax (*off*) Adèle!

There is a slight pause

Mrs Fairfax enters. She is an elderly woman of good bearing and kindly visage

Oh, that child is so excitable. Have you finished, Leah? It's getting very late.
Leah Yes, ma'am — just finished now.
Mrs Fairfax (*crossing to the archway*) You've placed flowers in the bedroom as I instructed? (*She looks in to inspect*)
Leah Yes, ma'am.
Mrs Fairfax Good. I see you've arranged things well. We must do all we can to make the young lady comfortable.
Leah Please, Mrs Fairfax — when's she comin', ma'am? Is it soon?

Mrs Fairfax John is meeting her in Milcote with the carriage. They should arrive very soon. You must prepare some hot soup — she will doubtless be fatigued by the long journey.

Leah Yes, ma'am. What about the master — should I prepare somethin' for 'um, ma'am?

Mrs Fairfax (*with a frown*) I really don't know if he will return this evening — he rode off very early this morning, but where I know not.

Leah Well, you never know with the master, do you ma'am?

Mrs Fairfax (*reproving*) No, Leah, you never know — but then it is not your business. The master has much work to do in controlling those estates and many other problems at home and abroad. It is your duty to keep things in a state of readiness for whenever he returns.

Leah Yes, ma'am. Ooh! We're all so excited about having a visitor — it's not often we see a new face at Thornfield.

Mrs Fairfax No, it isn't, Leah, but Miss Eyre is not a visitor as such. She will be Miss Adèle's new governess and you must treat her with due respect.

Leah I will, ma'am.

Mrs Fairfax Where did Miss Adèle go? Do you know?

Leah Perhaps in the garden, ma'am.

Mrs Fairfax Yes — she's hiding I'll be bound, lest she be put to bed before meeting her new governess.

Leah Yes, ma'am — she's so excited, too.

Mrs Fairfax She would be, poor mite. She's longing to converse in her own tongue. Her English is such that at times she cannot understand us, but Miss Eyre, I believe, speaks her language fluently.

Leah Oh well, she'll have no trouble then.

Mrs Fairfax No indeed. Can you see the child from the window, Leah? She mustn't run in the garden at this hour — she'll take cold.

Leah Yes, ma'am, there she is — I'll call ... (*She goes to open the window*)

Mrs Fairfax Do nothing of the kind — go down and fetch her, Leah. When will you learn?

Leah (*crossing to the door*) Sorry, ma'am.

Mrs Fairfax And bring her straight here.

Leah Yes, ma'am. (*She opens the double door*)

Grace Poole is standing immediately in the doorway

Leah gasps with surprise

Ooh, Mrs Poole — you frightened me.

Ignoring the girl, Mrs Poole enters the room silently. She is a middle-aged woman of striking appearance. One immediately feels that there is something

Act I, Scene 1 5

strange about this person; she is in complete contrast to Mrs Fairfax in appearance and manner

Mrs Fairfax What is it, Mrs Poole? Run along, Leah.

Leah exits

Mrs Poole (*ignoring the question and moving silently about the room*) The new lady's coming today then?
Mrs Fairfax Yes, that is correct. Why are you down here at this hour, Mrs Poole?
Mrs Poole New governess for the little one, eh? (*She utters a strange low chuckle as if at a secret thought*) That'll be a treat.
Mrs Fairfax If you have come merely to gossip, Mrs Poole, you must return upstairs and not neglect your duty.
Mrs Poole I only came down for a tray — it's the kitchen hands who neglect their duty. They've brought not a morsel since noon.
Mrs Fairfax Then go and see to your meal and don't concern yourself here.
Mrs Poole No, I won't — it's no concern of mine — not the new governess — I'll not be interested.
Mrs Fairfax Then go about your business.
Mrs Poole Why have you put her in these apartments?
Mrs Fairfax I have no choice — the master ordered it so.
Mrs Poole Wants to keep an eye on 'er, eh? From across the passage. (*She chuckles*) Well, that won't help. He's back now, but not for long I know — he'll be away across the seas in no time.
Mrs Fairfax That is not for you to say. The master will come and go as he pleases.

Adèle and Leah enter

Adèle Madame! Madame! Please — I stay to meet ma gouvernante — Please, madame — you allow me — please!
Mrs Fairfax Hush, child — do not be so excited — hush.
Leah I found her in the rose garden, ma'am.
Mrs Fairfax You've been hiding from us, haven't you child?
Adèle (*innocently*) Ooh, madame — je ne comprend pas — I do not understand ...
Mrs Fairfax Oh, I think you do. (*Laughing*) You're a naughty little girl.

Laughing happily, Adèle hugs Mrs Fairfax and swings around her

Adèle Oh, madame! (*She sees Mrs Poole for the first time*) Oh! Oh! Pardon, madame — I did not see you.

Mrs Poole (*after a slight pause, slowly*) She's a lively little thing, isn't she?
Mrs Fairfax If there is nothing more, Mrs Poole, please go back upstairs.
Mrs Poole All right — all right — I'm going. (*She stops at the door*) Goodbye, Miss Adèle.

Mrs Poole exits, chuckling

Adèle Oh, madame — 'oo is that lady? — she is not nice — she frightens me.
Mrs Fairfax Don't be silly, child — she is the sewing woman — she keeps our linen in good repair.
Adèle Why have I not seen her before — does she lives in the 'ouse?
Mrs Fairfax Yes, but she has her room high up in this wing and she is too busy to leave it often.
Adèle Oh!
Mrs Fairfax Now then, you must make ready for bed, Adèle.
Adèle Oh, madame — please ...
Mrs Fairfax And if you are a good girl you may come and meet your governess before you go to sleep.
Adèle Oh, merci madame — merci.
Mrs Fairfax But that is only if she arrives soon — do you understand?
Adèle Oh, madame.
Mrs Fairfax Now, Leah — take Miss Adèle to her room ——
Leah (*by the window*) Oh, ma'am, they are coming — the carriage is in the drive.
Adèle (*running to the window*) Oh, madame!
Leah It's at the door!
Adèle She is here, madame.
Mrs Fairfax (*laughing at their excitement*) All right — all right. Quickly, Leah, send Miss Adèle to her room and then bring Miss Eyre straight here.
Adèle Oh, madame — I wish to see ——
Mrs Fairfax When you are undressed you may come back. Go with Leah.

We hear the clanking of the front doorbell

Leah and Adèle exit L

John (*off*) This way, ma'am (*ad lib*).

Mrs Fairfax crosses to the doorway and looks uncertainly off to R. *With a worried frown she comes back into the room*

Leah appears in the doorway

Act I, Scene 1

Leah Miss Jane Eyre, ma'am.

Jane appears in the doorway. She is a girl of eighteen years, poorly but neatly dressed in a bonnet, shawl, black dress, etc. She is painfully thin and her features, though plain, show great strength of character

Jane How do you do, madam.
Mrs Fairfax You must have had a tedious ride. John drives so slowly — come and sit by the fire.
Jane Thank you. It was good of you to send the carriage. (*She sits*)
Mrs Fairfax Not at all, my dear. There is no carriage for hire in Milcote and it would be a long four miles to walk, would it not?
Jane Yes, indeed.
Mrs Fairfax And you have travelled many miles from Lowton today.
Jane Yes, it is a long way.

John enters bearing one small case and a box

Mrs Fairfax Ah, John — place Miss Eyre's luggage in her room.

John exits into the bedroom

This, I should explain, will be your sitting-room and classroom, Miss Eyre, and adjoining there is your private apartment.

Jane stands up

Please do not disturb yourself now: there is time enough to see your room after you have taken refreshment.
Jane (*sitting*) Thank you.
Mrs Fairfax It is not spacious, but I thought you would like it better than one of the large front chambers. They are so dreary and solitary: we never use them unless we have company.
Jane Thank you for your consideration.
Mrs Fairfax The rest of the wing we do not use, not above this landing. There is just one servant's room up there so you will not need to use those stairs.
Jane I understand.

John enters from the bedroom

Mrs Fairfax John, you can store Miss Eyre's box tomorrow when she has had time to unpack.
John Yes, ma'am.

Mrs Fairfax And do tell Leah to ...

Leah enters carrying a tray with soup, etc.

Ah, there you are, Leah.
Leah The soup, ma'am.
Mrs Fairfax Good.
Mrs Fairfax Thank you, Leah, you may go.
Leah Yes, ma'am.

Leah and John exit

Jane Mmm, it is very good.
Mrs Fairfax It will warm you.

There is a slight pause

Jane Will I have the pleasure of seeing Miss Fairfax this evening?
Mrs Fairfax Miss Fairfax? Oh, I see — you mean Miss Varens. Varens is the name of your pupil — Adèle Varens.
Jane Then she is not your daughter?
Mrs Fairfax Oh, no — I have no family.
Jane Then I beg your pardon. Since it was your letter that I received I assumed that it was your daughter.
Mrs Fairfax Oh, bless you, no. Adèle is the ward of Mr Rochester ...
Jane Mr Rochester?
Mrs Fairfax The master of this house and, indeed, the surrounding estates.
Jane Oh — I — I thought that you were the owner of this house.
Mrs Fairfax Oh no, my dear. I am merely the housekeeper for Mr Rochester, but since he travels a great deal I am responsible for all manner of details.
Jane I understand now. Tell me — how long have you held the post?
Mrs Fairfax Oh, for many years now. I served old Mr Rochester until he died some nine summers past. Mr Edward was abroad at that time, but he returned to take up the inheritance.
Jane Mrs Fairfax, you told me in your letter that Miss Adèle has lived for most of her life in France.
Mrs Fairfax Yes, that is so. She is a sweet child, but her background has been unsettled, I believe. Mr Rochester has made her his ward since her family died and she was left all alone. He brought her to England a few months ago. I know but little of her circumstances.
Jane Her English, you said, was poor. How have you dealt with the problem? Do you speak the French tongue?

Act I, Scene 1

Mrs Fairfax No, I fear not — but since she has been here her vocabulary has greatly improved. You will, no doubt, have little difficulty in her tutorage — she seems a bright child.
Jane That is good.
Mrs Fairfax You have been teaching in a charitable institution, I believe?
Jane Yes — Lowood School. I taught there for three years and before that I was a pupil at the same establishment.
Mrs Fairfax And did they treat you well?
Jane Some did. (*There is a slight pause*)
Mrs Fairfax Well, now, my dear, you are among friends. We will look after you.
Jane You are most kind.
Mrs Fairfax Would you care for a little more soup? Oh, but look child, you haven't had your sandwich — you must be hungry.
Jane Thank you, but I have a small appetite.
Mrs Fairfax Well, we must definitely improve that state of affairs. You are so painfully thin...

Jane smiles

Adèle bursts into the room followed by Leah

Adèle Madame! Madame! I am as you have told me; please may I come in?
Mrs Fairfax (*laughing*) It seems that you are already in. (*To Jane*) I promised her that she might see you before going to sleep. She's been so excited about your arrival. Adèle — come and speak to the lady who is to teach you and to make you a clever young woman one day.
Adèle Bon soir, madame — Bon soir — Je suis enchanté de vous voir...
Jane Bon soir, Adèle. Comment vous portez-vous?
Adèle Oh, madame, je suis très bien — mais oui — très bien ...
Mrs Fairfax Enough, Adèle — you must speak English — that is to be our first task — to improve your English tongue.
Adèle Yes, mademoiselle.
Jane Where was it that you lived in France, Adèle?
Adèle Paris, mam'selle. I lived in Paris with my mamma.
Jane I have heard much of that city. I believe it is very beautiful.
Adèle Ah, oui, mam'selle — it was lovely there with my mamma, but she is gone now to the Holy Virgin and I am all alone.
Mrs Fairfax Oh, no Adèle, you must not say that. We are all your friends here, aren't we, Miss Eyre?
Jane Why yes, of course. You and I, Adèle, will have lovely times together. You can tell me all about Paris and your life there and...

Adèle Ah oui. In Paris, Mamma used to teach me to sing and dance and to say verses and then a great many ladies and gentlemen would come and see Mamma and I would sing for them. Would you like me to sing for you now?
Mrs Fairfax I think it is late now, Adèle.
Jane Yes, it is, too late now, Adèle. Tomorrow we will talk and you will show me all that you have learned.
Mrs Fairfax Leah, take the child to her room now. Say good-night, Adèle.
Adèle Bon nuit, mademoiselle.
Jane Good-night, Adèle.
Adèle Good-night, mademoiselle. Good-night, madame.
Mrs Fairfax Good-night, my dear, and God bless you, child.

Leah and Adèle exit

Jane She seems a well-mannered child.
Mrs Fairfax Oh yes, but excitable. I think there has been a certain lack of discipline in her life. Her mother, it seems, was an artist in the theatre — such an unsettling background.
Jane What of her father?
Mrs Fairfax I have never heard mention of him. I'm afraid I've told you all I know.
Jane Has Mr Rochester not told you of him?
Mrs Fairfax I'm afraid Mr Rochester does not readily impart information, and one would never presume to ask.
Jane I beg your pardon, Mrs Fairfax, if I appear inquisitive, I only wished to ——
Mrs Fairfax Nonsense, my dear. Your interest is only natural, but Mr Rochester is — well — you will judge for yourself when you meet him.
Jane You make a mystery, Mrs Fairfax. Shall I meet him today?
Mrs Fairfax That I do not know. I would say it is improbable at this late hour. Do not let me worry you, my dear. Mr Rochester is a strange man in many ways, but he is a good master — that I will say. And now, my dear, you must be tired and anxious to settle your belongings.
Jane Yes, indeed. (*She stands*)
Mrs Fairfax Oh, dear — the girl has forgotten to bring your candle. Wait, and I will get you one for your room.
Jane Thank you.

Mrs Fairfax exits to L

Jane moves about the room inspecting it properly for the first time. We hear the wind rising as she nears the window and as she stands surveying the darkened panorama outside, a violent gust of wind blows open the window

Act I, Scene 1   11

sending the curtains flapping. Jane, quickly recovering from the surprise, makes fast the window in time to hear from within the house, off R, *a wild hysterical laugh. She runs to open the door*

(*Calling*) Mrs Fairfax! Mrs Fairfax!

Mrs Fairfax appears in the doorway, an anxious expression on her face. She holds an unlighted candle

Mrs Fairfax I am here, child.
Jane What was that? That strange laugh? (*She is more concerned than frightened*)
Mrs Fairfax Yes — yes, my dear ...
Jane What was it? Did you not hear it?
Mrs Fairfax My dear, it was just one of the servants — do not distress yourself.
Jane But it sounded so ... so strange.
Mrs Fairfax It was nothing. Probably it was Mrs Poole. She is our sewing woman and has the room above. I must speak to her — so much noise at this hour. It is nothing more, I am sure.
Jane It startled me, that's all.
Mrs Fairfax You're just tired after your journey and a little on edge, I expect.
Jane Yes, I'm sure you are right.
Mrs Fairfax Here is your candle. Now, are you sure you will be comfortable?
Jane Oh yes — yes, thank you.
Mrs Fairfax Well, I'll leave you then. Do sleep well, child.
Jane I'm sure I will. Thank you for your kindness to me.
Mrs Fairfax It is nothing. I'm very glad that you have come. I do hope you'll be happy here. Good-night to you.
Jane Good-night, Mrs Fairfax.

Mrs Fairfax exits

Jane lights the candle on the table and takes it with her as she exits to the bedroom. After a second, she appears with a plain flannel nightdress

She moves to the main door and cautiously inspects the darkened passage. Satisfied, she crosses to the fire where she briefly warms her hands before unlacing her black dress and stepping out of it. Jane casts a look around the room, an expression of obvious happiness upon her face. She sets an eye on the wall immediately above the window and taking her shawl about her shoulders she crosses to the crucifix that hangs there. In a second she kneels

Dear Lord, I thank thee for my deliverance to this haven. May I deserve the good things that lie in store for me and may I work and earn the respect of my employers and the love of my neighbours. May I not err in my duty to this house and my duty to thee. Amen. Our Father, which art in Heaven, hallowed be Thy name. Thy kingdom come, Thy will be done ...

At this moment the door C bursts open and Rochester stands in the doorway. He is dressed in a long black riding cloak and carries a crop

Jane rises, frightened, and steps back to the window

Rochester Forgive me, madame — I interrupt your prayers, it seems.
Jane Mr — Mr Rochester, is it not?
Rochester Remarkably clever of you, young woman, but I fear you have me at a disadvantage. What is the reason for your presence in this house?
Jane I have come to be your ward's governess.
Rochester Deuce take me if I had not forgotten! (*He enters the room*) The governess, eh? I understand. The date of your arrival had escaped me ... What is your name?
Jane Jane Eyre.
Rochester Very well, Jane Eyre. Come into the light that I might see that which is to cost me thirty pounds a year. Come — what are you afraid of?

Jane does so. He stares at her intently for a second

Hmm! Where have you come from?
Jane From Lowood School, near Lowton, sir.
Rochester Ah yes — a charitable concern. How long were you there?
Jane Eight years.
Rochester Eight years? No wonder you have rather the look of another world. Half the time in such a place would have done up any constitution! Who are your parents?
Jane I have none, sir.
Rochester Nor ever had, I suppose?
Jane No, sir.
Rochester Have you kinsfolk? Aunts? Uncles?
Jane None.
Rochester And your home?
Jane I do not have one, sir.
Rochester Then where were you born?
Jane I know not, sir, but when I was but a few months old my parents died of the typhus fever and I was taken in by my uncle ...
Rochester Uncle? You said that you had none.

Act I, Scene 1

Jane That uncle is dead these many years and his wife ...

Slight pause

Rochester What of his wife?
Jane (*quietly*) I once said I would never call her aunt again.
Rochester Oh! What mystery is this? What secret villainy is here?
Jane There is no reason for jest, sir.
Rochester What? Do I hear you reproving me?
Jane With respect, sir — I thought you were mocking me. My life with Mrs Reed, my uncle's wife, was most unhappy and when I was ten years of age I was sent away to Lowood School.
Rochester And you stayed there for eight years. You are now then eighteen?
Jane Yes, sir.
Rochester Arithmetic, you see, is useful. And what did they teach you in this institution? Have you read much?
Jane Only the books that came my way and they have not been numerous or very learned.
Rochester Have you seen much society?
Jane None but the pupils and teachers of Lowood.
Rochester You have lived the life of a nun. No doubt you are well drilled in religious forms. Brocklehurst, who directs Lowood, I believe, is a clergyman, is he not?
Jane Yes, sir.
Rochester And I suppose you girls worshipped him?
Jane Oh, no, sir.
Rochester No? What, a novice not worship her priest? This sounds blasphemous.
Jane I disliked Mr Brocklehurst and was not alone in that feeling, sir. He is a harsh man, pompous and meddling. He starved us and cut off our hair and lectured us so often on sudden deaths and judgments that we were afraid to sleep in our beds.
Rochester What a number of enemies you have found in your young life. Could it be that you were an ungrateful child — so ungrateful to your aunt while she was your benefactor that she was forced to send you to Lowood?
Jane No, sir. That is not true ...
Rochester And again at Lowood, where you were sheltered and cared for, guided and tutored, perhaps you were ill-mannered and badly behaved and deserved the just punishment.
Jane You are ill-informed, sir. I was never accepted in Mrs Reed's house. My uncle, I am told, made my aunt promise to bring me up with his own children as their equal, but I was treated as a servant girl. And at Lowood School I was not alone in suffering what you have termed punishments.

Indeed, they were part of the school curriculum. Happily, in recent years, Mr Brocklehurst has been relieved of certain duties and conditions have greatly improved.
Rochester A most impressive speech. Perhaps I have wronged you after all. You are a creature of spirit — a compensation for your unprepossessing appearance. You may retire now — doubtless we will meet again.

Rochester exits as——

——the CURTAIN *falls*

SCENE 2

The same. January 1847

As the CURTAIN *rises we see a few minor changes in the room. The furniture has been slightly re-arranged and Jane is sitting with Adèle at the table that now stands in the window area. On the table are various drawing materials and painting equipment, together with a large portfolio containing several sketches and paintings*

Jane Adèle, you are still holding your pencil incorrectly — again I must tell you.
Adèle Mademoiselle?
Jane You must rest your forefinger lightly — so — (*She resets the pencil in Adèle's hand*) Do not clasp it so tightly or your hand will not be relaxed and the lines of your drawing will not flow freely.
Adèle Excusez-moi, mademoiselle.
Jane In English, Adèle.
Adèle I am sorry, Miss Aire.
Jane That is better.
Adèle Is the drawing bad, mademoiselle?
Jane It is not good, Adèle, but I think there is a little improvement.
Adèle Oh, thank you — thank you, mam'selle — I am glad.
Jane You must continue to try hard.
Adèle I will, mam'selle, but is it time for me to go yet? I have to have my tea and change my clothes.
Jane Not quite time yet, Adèle ...
Adèle But Monsieur Rochester is coming and I must be ready.
Jane There is plenty of time, Adèle — you must not get excited.
Adèle But he has been away to Paris and whenever he returns from travelling he always brings a cadeau...

Act I, Scene 2   15

Jane Present, Adèle. Present.
Adèle (*with effort*) Yes — present. (*She laughs*) "He presents me with the present!"
Jane (*laughing*) That's right.
Adèle Oh, mam'selle — 'e brings me back lovely things ——
Jane Yes — yes — but we must still finish our lessons. Now I want you to colour this sketch.

Mrs Fairfax enters

Mrs Fairfax Ah, you are still working, I see.
Jane Yes, Mrs Fairfax.
Mrs Fairfax I'm sorry to interrupt you, my dear, but I would like Adèle to take tea early today as Mr Rochester is returning.
Adèle Oui, madame — I have said this. I must be pretty for monsieur.
Jane (*smiling*) She has talked of nothing else all day.
Adèle May I go, mam'selle?
Jane Well, it seems I am beaten. Very well, Adèle, but we must make up for this tomorrow.
Adèle Oui, mam'selle, oui — I will work very 'ard tomorrow.
Jane All right then. Clear the paints away and put your picture on the table.
Adèle Oui, mam'selle.
Mrs Fairfax I am so sorry, my dear, if I have upset your lessons.
Jane Of course you haven't, Mrs Fairfax. She is too excited to work well today in any case.
Mrs Fairfax Ah yes. Adèle, when you have done, go straight to Leah and she will give you your tea.
Adèle Oui, madame.
Mrs Fairfax I've had such a time today — preparing for Mr Rochester's home-coming. I only received his letter this morning. It had been delayed.
Adèle May I go now, please mam'selle?
Jane Yes, Adèle.
Adèle Merci, mam'selle.

Adèle exits

Jane Mr Rochester has been in France then?
Mrs Fairfax Yes, according to the letter. He spends a great deal of time there, on business I believe.
Jane I have only seen him on the one occasion, the day of my arrival here last October.
Mrs Fairfax Of course. He left early that following morning.
Jane He seemed to be a man of strange moods.

Mrs Fairfax Yes, I don't know how long he will stay this time, but you will doubtless see more of him. He will be most anxious for a report of Miss Adèle's progress, I'm sure.
Jane He must be very fond of her.
Mrs Fairfax I think he is, but in a strange way. Her actual presence annoys him at times.
Jane But how can that be? She is a sweet child and seems to love him much.
Mrs Fairfax I know — but somehow her embraces seem to irritate him. He never seems at ease with her. There is no accounting for it.
Jane But perhaps he will stay longer this time and come to relax in her company.
Mrs Fairfax I do hope so. It would be a good thing. He's such a restless soul. One day I hope that he will settle here for good — perhaps even take a wife.
Jane Is there a lady in whom he shows interest?
Mrs Fairfax Well, it was rumoured that he had formed an attachment with old Lord Ingram's daughter, but nothing seems to have come of it.
Jane The Ingrams? They have an estate nearby, do they not?
Mrs Fairfax Yes, some twenty miles away. She is a beautiful young woman. I remember when she came here to a Christmas ball and party, seven years ago it must be. You should have seen the dining-room that day, how richly it was decorated, how brilliantly lit up. I should think there were fifty ladies and gentlemen present. All of the first county families, and Miss Ingram was considered the belle of the evening.
Jane What is she like? You say beautiful?
Mrs Fairfax Yes, tall and graceful with eyes large and dark, and such fine hair. She was dressed that evening in pure white with an amber-coloured scarf passed over her shoulder. She was greatly admired.
Jane And she is not yet married?
Mrs Fairfax Not as yet. I fancy neither she nor her sister has a very large fortune.
Jane But that surely would not stand in a gentleman's way. Mr Rochester, for instance — he is rich, is he not?
Mrs Fairfax Yes, but of course there is a considerable difference in age. She is but twenty-five years ...

Leah enters excitedly

Leah Mrs Fairfax — Mrs Fairfax — the master's here.
Rochester (*off*) John! John! Where are you, man?
Mrs Fairfax I must go. Leah — downstairs quickly.

Leah exits

Mrs Fairfax moves to the passageway

Act I, Scene 2

John (*off*) Sorry, sir. I didn't know you were here, sir.
Rochester (*off*) Get the bags, man.
Mrs Fairfax (*from the passageway outside*) Good-evening, sir. Welcome home.
Rochester (*off*) A fine welcome I receive.

Rochester appears in the passageway

The servants gossiping and absent from their duties.
Mrs Fairfax I'm sorry, sir. We did not expect you as yet.
Rochester (*opening door to his room*) John! Where are you, man?
John (*off*) Coming, sir!
Mrs Fairfax What time would you like dinner, sir?
Rochester Not yet — not yet. (*He turns, looking into the library for the first time*) What's this? My library turned upside down? (*He enters the room and sees Jane*) Ah yes, of course, the governess.
Jane Good-evening, sir.
Rochester Good-evening. I see you have turned my library into a regular classroom.
Jane I was instructed to use this room for the purpose. I hope you do not disapprove of the arrangements, sir.
Rochester Do as you wish, young woman, so long as you teach that troublesome child a thing or two. All right, Mrs Fairfax — I'm sure you have many things to do.

John appears in the passageway and enters Rochester's room with his bags

Mrs Fairfax Yes, sir. Do you wish that your luggage be unpacked?
Rochester No, leave it, Mrs Fairfax, please. I would prefer to muddle things in my own way. (*He approaches the table and casually inspects the portfolio*) Take my cloak, though, if you will.
Mrs Fairfax (*coming forward*) Yes, sir. Shall I have tea brought to you?
Rochester Tea, Mrs Fairfax, I find most refreshing on occasion, but at this moment a glass of brandy would be more in order.
Mrs Fairfax Brandy, sir?
Rochester Yes, Mrs Fairfax. My stomach has not yet recovered from the turbulence of the channel.
Mrs Fairfax Very well, sir.

Mrs Fairfax exits

Rochester watches her exit, then laughs, suddenly and uproariously. Just as suddenly he stops and addresses Jane

Rochester She does not approve, I think. Brandy at this hour is not in Mrs Fairfax's book it would seem. (*He looks at Jane quizzically*) You prefer not to comment, Miss ——
Jane My name is Eyre, sir.
Rochester Ah, yes. I remember. (*Turning to the portfolio*) You have been sketching, Miss Eyre?
Jane Yes, sir. May I show you some of Adèle's drawings? She shows great improvement.
Rochester These are examples of your work presumably, Miss Eyre?
Jane Yes, sir. I would like to ...
Rochester Do not chatter, Miss Eyre.

She stops, open-mouthed

Mmm. A master aided you with these, I think.
Jane No, indeed, sir.
Rochester (*looking up*) Oh! I see that pricks your pride. (*Returning his gaze to the pictures*) And when did you find time to do them? They have taken much time and some thought.
Jane I did them in the last two vacations I spent at Lowood, when I had no other duty.
Rochester I see — and were you happy when you painted these pictures?
Jane Yes, sir. I was happy. I have found that in painting I derive my keenest pleasure.
Rochester That is not to say very much. Your pleasures from your own account have been few, if I remember correctly. Yes, these pictures are quite rare for one so young. I think you have secured at least the shadow of your thoughts, but you had not artist's skill and science to give them full being. Yet the drawings are for a schoolgirl, peculiar. As to the thoughts, they are elfish. Who taught you to paint the wind?

Adèle runs into the room followed by Leah who appears with a brandy decanter and glass

Adèle Bon soir, monsieur — bon soir!
Rochester Control yourself, child: do not enter the room at such a gallop.
Adèle Pardon, monsieur. I am so excited to see you.
Rochester Excited to see me? I think you are more excited at the prospect of a present than the sight of your ferocious guardian. Thank you, Leah.

Leah places the brandy on a side table and exits

Adèle "Present", monsieur? (*Innocently*) What is that?

Act I, Scene 2

Rochester Do you not know the word, Adèle?
Adèle (*wide-eyed*) No, sir.
Jane Do not be deceitful, Adèle. You know the word quite well.
Rochester Oh, do not be hard on the child, Miss Eyre. It seems that her vocabulary does not contain the word, and if that is so, she can hardly be disappointed at not receiving its definition.
Adèle Oh, monsieur, it is a cadeau. I remember, a cadeau ——
Rochester Ah, she remembers, Miss Eyre.
Adèle Have you a cadeau for me, m'sieur? Have you?
Rochester What is this talk of cadeaux: I have no cadeau for you.
Adèle Have you a cadeau for Miss Eyre, sir?
Rochester I have no cadeau for anyone: a present, perhaps, but for Miss Eyre? Did you expect a present, madame? Are you fond of presents?
Jane I hardly know, sir. I have little experience of them. They are generally thought pleasant things, I believe.
Rochester Generally thought? But what do you think?
Jane I think it is your custom to bring playthings for Adèle, but I am just a stranger and have done nothing to deserve acknowledgment.
Rochester You are being over modest. You have obviously taken great pains with Adèle in teaching her our language. I notice great improvement.
Jane You have given me my cadeau, sir. It is the mead all teachers covet most — praise of their pupil's progress.
Rochester Hmm. Adèle, you may go to my room and at the top of my black valise you will find a box.
Adèle (*hugging him excitedly*) Oh, m'sieur — merci — merci!
Rochester (*irritated*) All right — all right — enough — take the box, you true daughter of Paris, and amuse yourself with disembowelling it.
Adèle Merci, merci, monsieur.

Adèle exits

Rochester (*with a sigh*) I am not fond of the prattle of children, and she ... but no matter.

He sits with glass of brandy and notices that Jane is still standing

Sit down, Miss Eyre, you're hovering like a servant.
Jane (*quietly*) I am a servant, sir.
Rochester Then do as you are told. I am sorry, Miss Eyre, you must excuse my tone of command, but I am used to saying "do this" and it is done. I cannot alter my customary habits for one new inmate.

Jane sits and watches him intently as he sips from his brandy

Rochester You examine me, Miss Eyre. Do you think me handsome?
Jane (*surprised at the question and answering automatically*) No, sir... I — I mean ...
Rochester Hmm! A speedy reply which if not blunt, is at least brusque. What do you mean by it?
Jane Sir, I was too plain. I beg your pardon.
Rochester But I do not grant it. You must explain.
Jane I — I ought to have replied that it was not easy to give an impromptu answer to a question about appearances, that tastes differ and that beauty is of little consequence...
Rochester You ought to have replied no such thing. Beauty of little consequence indeed? But no — go on. What fault do you find in me, pray?
Jane Mr Rochester, allow me to disown my first answer. It was a foolish blunder.
Rochester Just so — and you shall answer for it. Criticize me. (*Whimsically*) Does my forehead not please you? It is broad and shaped, according to common belief, to denote the fact that I bear a conscience — even a rude tenderness of the heart.
Jane I see that, sir ...
Rochester These features of my character were possibly more obvious when I was a child of your years but fortune has knocked me about a good deal — I now must flatter myself that I am as hard and as tough as this very table!
Jane I — I would ... (*Slight pause*)
Rochester Yes?
Jane It was but a thought, sir.
Rochester Then voice it, Miss Eyre.
Jane I would prefer not to, sir.
Rochester Do not be afraid, Miss Eyre. I am in quite a kindly mood this evening. I haven't slayed a single person all day.

Jane smiles at this

What's this? A smile, Miss Eyre? I would not have thought it possible. But continue, please.
Jane It was merely an impulse to say that the qualities you have described are not always subjects for flattery, in my opinion.
Rochester A worthy opinion, of course, Miss Eyre. But perhaps I am not all strength and metal. I may well be pervious through a chink or two here and there. Does this leave hope for me, in your opinion?

Jane is mystified. He looks at her, then laughs

You look most puzzled, Miss Eyre, and though you are not pretty any more than I am handsome, a puzzled air becomes you.

Act I, Scene 2

Jane (*quietly*) You are generous, sir.

Rochester You can never accuse me of that, young woman. Why the very fact that I am here with you now is proof of my great selfishness. I am disposed to be communicative and gregarious tonight and I find the firelight and the brandy decanter insufficient company for me. You, I find, an adequate substitute.

Jane I think you make me a figure of fun, sir.

Rochester And what is wrong with that — a very worthy occupation indeed. But no, you are wrong. You puzzled me that first evening, and I am interested to learn more of you — therefore, speak.

Jane (*grimly*) I think, sir, that you would find me an inadequate substitute for the decanter and unworthy of your society.

Slight pause

Rochester Miss Eyre, I beg your pardon. I put my request in an absurd, insolent form. The fact is I do not wish to treat you like an inferior — that is, I claim only such superiority as must result from twenty years difference in age, and a century's advance in experience. Do you agree that I should make such a claim?

Jane You must do as you please, sir.

Rochester That is no answer, Miss Eyre.

Jane I don't think, sir, you have the right to command me merely because you are older than I, or because you have seen more of the world than I have. Your claim to superiority depends on the use you have made of your time and experience.

Rochester (*slightly startled and amused*) I see. Then leaving superiority out of the question, you must still agree to receive my orders now and then without being piqued or hurt at the tone of command. (*Quite sincerely*) Will you?

Jane smiles

You smile again?

Jane I was thinking, sir, that very few masters would trouble themselves to enquire whether or not their paid subordinates were piqued and hurt by their orders.

Rochester Paid subordinates? Oh yes, I remember the salary. But still on that mercenary ground, will you agree to let me hector you a little?

Jane No sir, not on that ground, but on the ground that you care whether or not a dependant is comfortable in her dependency, I agree heartily.

Rochester You have found virtue, Miss Eyre. I congratulate you. I thought there were only faults.

Jane There surely must be both in every man.

Rochester In the course of your future life you will often find yourself elected involuntary confidante of your acquaintances' secrets. People will always instinctively know that you are a listener; they will find you a person of innate sympathy. You, Miss Eyre, will hear the troubles of the world.
Jane I think perhaps, that in time, sir, I might change — with experience of more society.
Rochester Yes, yes, it is possible — the Lowood restraint still clings to you, of course, controlling your features and muffling your voice. I see at intervals the glance of a curious sort of bird through the close-set bars of a cage: a vivid restless, resolute captive is there; were it but free, it would soar cloud-high. You never laugh, Miss Eyre!
Jane Perhaps there are occasions, sir.
Rochester I hope so.

Adèle enters wearing a pink silk frock

Adèle M'sieur, m'sieur, it is beautiful, beautiful, my cadeau. Mam'selle, ma robe, voilà. (*She pirouettes*) Oh, merci, m'sieur. (*She hugs and kisses Rochester*)
Jane Oh, how pretty it is.
Rochester All right, child.
Adèle I will dance for you, m'sieur. Watch me, m'sieur. Watch! Just like Mamma — watch! (*She pirouettes and dances a few steps, laughing*)

Rochester rises, staring at the child, his face is tense

Rochester (*suddenly*) Adèle! (*Thundering*) Stop this. Stop.

Adèle is still immediately and very frightened

Leave the room and take off that dress.
Adèle But m'sieur. My present ...
Rochester I never want to see you wearing that dress again. Do you understand.
Adèle Oui, m'sieur.
Rochester Then go.

Adèle quickly and quietly exits

There is a pause. Then Jane hurriedly starts collecting her paintings together and replacing them in her portfolio

Act I, Scene 2

(*Quietly*) I must beg your pardon, Miss Eyre. My behaviour must seem strange to you.
Jane It is not for me to criticize, sir.
Rochester But you think, nevertheless, that I am unkind to the child.
Jane You force me to agree with you, sir.

There is a pause. Rochester pours brandy

Rochester The explanation is simple, Miss Eyre. I bought the dress for Adèle as I knew it would make her happy — but — I was totally unprepared for her appearance in it.
Jane I am afraid I do not understand, sir.
Rochester Then I'd best explain. Adèle's mother was a French opera-dancer towards whom I once cherished a *grande* passion which she professed to return. I was young and believed her. I gave her everything — jewels, a carriage, cloths of cashmere and gold. I would have given her the world were it possible. In short I began the process of my ruin.
Jane What happened?
Rochester I had — I deserved to have the fate of any young infatuated fool. The object of my love proved unworthy of such affection and one day I arrived to find her in the arms of another. You would think it ended there — but no! Unluckily, six months earlier she had given birth to Adèle who she assured me was my daughter, though I saw no proof of resemblance written in her countenance. Some years later she abandoned the child and ran away. Now, Jane, although I acknowledge no claim on Adèle's part to be supported by me, hearing that she was destitute, I took the poor thing out of the slime and mud of Paris and brought her here to grow up clean and wholesome. I shock you Miss Eyre, but it is true. Her mother took my money and was unfaithful to me but Adèle was already in existence. Now that you know that she is the bastard offspring of a French opera girl, you will perhaps think differently about your protégée.
Jane No sir. Adèle is not answerable for either her mother's faults or yours. And now that I know she is, in a sense, parentless, I shall cling to her closer than before.
Rochester Oh, that is the light in which you view it. (*After a pause, moving to the door*) Would you care to dine with me, Miss Eyre?
Jane It is most kind of you, sir, but I have little appetite this evening. I would only take a hot drink before retiring.
Rochester As you wish. Is it perhaps my confessions which have robbed you of your appetite?
Jane (*smiling gently*) Oh no, sir. I quite often do not take dinner and tonight I am tired and will retire early.
Rochester Then I will wish you good-night.

Jane Good-night sir. Thank you.
Rochester Thank you, for your society.

Rochester exits and slowly Jane turns and goes into her room

The Lights fade to Black-out. Music

Scene 3

The same. Five hours later

Slowly the flicker of the fire appears in the grate and the sound of wind rises over the music bridge which now fades

Suddenly there is a sound of hysterical laughter, the slamming of a door and footsteps hurriedly ascending the stairs

In a second Jane appears in the doorway of her bedroom, clutching a shawl around her shoulders. She pauses and then moves quickly to the door leading to Rochester's room, from which smoke is curling

Jane Mr Rochester! Mr Rochester! (*She struggles with the door which is locked*) Mr Rochester ... wake up ... quickly ... there's fire!!

The door opens and Jane rushes in and grabs a jug of water which she throws over Rochester. Overcome by the smoke, he staggers out, followed by Jane

Rochester In the name of all the elves in Christendom what have you done? Have you plotted to drown me?
Jane Sir, your room was on fire. Thank God you are all right.

Rochester stumbles

Let me help you.
Rochester I am all right, Jane, but the bed curtains are still alight. Water.

Rochester exits to his room and returns almost immediately to Jane in the passageway

It is out now.
Jane Are you sure? There is still so much smoke.

Act I, Scene 4

Rochester It will clear. If you hadn't woken me the whole house could have caught fire.

They move into the library

Jane Sir, I saw a candlestick on the floor.
Rochester It must have fallen there as I slept. A careless accident.
Jane An accident that might have been fatal, sir. Are you recovered?
Rochester I think a little brandy will complete the cure. (*He sits*) Jane, tell me, what made you open your chamber door?
Jane It was a laugh, sir. A wild frightening laugh that awakened me.
Rochester Have you heard this laugh before?
Jane Yes, sir. There is a woman here called Grace Poole. She laughs that way. She is a singular person.
Rochester Just so, Jane. Grace Poole — you have guessed it. She is, as you say, singular, very singular. Well, I shall reflect on the subject. Meantime I am glad that you are the only person besides myself acquainted with the precise details of tonight's incident. Say nothing about it. I will account for this state of affairs. Now Jane, you must sleep.
Jane Yes, sir.
Rochester I knew you would do me good in some way, at some time — I knew it when I first saw you. You have saved my life, snatched me from a horrible death and from this moment I owe you an immense debt. I cannot say more.
Jane There is no debt sir, no obligation. Good-night, sir.
Rochester Good-night, Jane.

She exits

My cherished preserver. (*He stares after her. Then, throwing off certain thoughts he quickly strides to the double doors*)

He pauses momentarily as he looks upstairs, then starts to ascend the staircase and exits

CURTAIN

SCENE 4

The same. April, 1847

When the CURTAIN *rises Leah is hurriedly but ineffectually tidying the room*

John enters

John Oh, there you are, Leah. Mrs Fairfax wants you in the kitchen as soon as you've done.
Leah All right — I haven't nearly finished yet. There's too much to do with the house full. I've only got one pair of hands...
John I know — it's all these visitors.
Leah I can't do everything.
John The mistress says she's had to get rid of one of the extra girls.
Leah Oh, not another one. Big house party like this — you've got to have extra 'ands.
John What's it all about anyway? We 'aven't 'ad company at Thornfield for years — I was a lad ...
Leah (*knowingly*) I think it's all to do with Miss Ingram.
John What do you mean?
Leah Ah, well. (*Smugly*) Ah, well.
John Well, don't just stand there saying "Ah, well". What you talking about?
Leah You 'aven't been watching, 'ave you?
John Watching what?
Leah 'Er and the master.
John Well, what about them?
Leah Getting married, that's what.
John Married? Them?
Leah Yes, the engagement's going to be announced any time now.
John How do you know?
Leah Well, it stands to reason — that's why all these guests are staying. They always do it like this. Have a big 'ouseparty and then they tell everyone.
John Mmm. Well, she's a comely wench anyway.
Leah Ooh, listen to you, talking about Miss Ingram like that!
John Well, I'm right, aren't I? He's picked a nice 'un there.
Leah Oh, she's very beautiful I must say — but very 'igh and mighty.
John Well, good luck to 'em anyway.
Leah He's been much better tempered lately, I'll say that. Help me with this, John.

They move the table

John Right ...
Leah Careful.

Some papers slip from the table

Oh, you clumsy thing — all Miss Eyre's papers.
John No harm done.
Leah Be quick — pick them up, and put 'em away.

Act I, Scene 4

John *She's gone out, 'asn't she?*
Leah Yes, out walking again. She walks for hours these evenings.
John She's a funny little thing.
Leah She's been very quiet lately.
John 'Ow d'you mean?
Leah Mmm, well, I think she's heard the goings-on.
John Upstairs?
Leah Yes.
John Does she know?
Leah No, I don't think so.
John Oh, well, p'raps it's better that way.
Leah P'raps it is.

Mrs Fairfax enters

Mrs Fairfax Ah, Leah, if you've finished please go and help Cook. Dinner is being served, but the new hands are very bad.
Leah Yes, ma'am.
Mrs Fairfax And John, would you take a tray up to Mrs Poole?
John Yes, ma'am.

John exits

Leah is collecting her cleaning materials

Mrs Fairfax Thank goodness the child is to bed early this evening. Miss Eyre is out still, is she, Leah?
Leah Yes, ma'am.
Mrs Fairfax Well, when you see her, tell her I have a message for her will you?
Leah (*curiously*) A message, ma'am?
Mrs Fairfax Yes, Leah, a message for Miss Eyre, not for you, so do not be inquisitive.
Leah No, ma'am.
Mrs Fairfax Go and help Cook like a good girl.
Leah Yes, ma'am. (*She goes to the passageway*) Oh, here's Miss Eyre now, ma'am.
Mrs Fairfax All right, Leah.
Leah Mrs Fairfax is here, Miss Eyre.

Jane enters, wearing her cloak, and Leah exits

Mrs Fairfax Good-evening, my dear.

Jane Good-evening.

Mrs Fairfax You've been walking again. You really must take care. These evenings are still cold.

Jane A long walk is most healthy, Mrs Fairfax, provided one dresses warmly. (*She removes her cloak*)

Mrs Fairfax Well, perhaps you are right.

Jane Have the company dined yet?

Mrs Fairfax Yes, they are just finishing. They are later tonight because Miss Ingram and Mr Rochester have been riding and have only recently returned.

Jane Oh, I see.

Mrs Fairfax They've been out together for hours today. You know, I think that they might marry after all.

Jane From what I have seen he admires her greatly.

Mrs Fairfax Yes, and she him, I would think. They haven't been apart these past few days.

Jane I have only seen her briefly, but she is very beautiful.

Mrs Fairfax Well, you will see more of her this evening. Mr Rochester has asked that you join the guests in the drawing-room after dinner.

Jane Me? But for what reason?

Mrs Fairfax Well, I presume that he wishes you to add to the company.

Jane But why? It is a week since the guests arrived and I have not been required before. Please, Mrs Fairfax — surely it is not necessary?

Mrs Fairfax Well, I did remind Mr Rochester that you were unused to company and that I didn't think that you would be at ease in such a party of gentry but he insisted.

Jane Oh, you were quite right, Mrs Fairfax. I would prefer not to attend. Will you make my excuses?

Mrs Fairfax The master will not take kindly to your refusal, but I will do what I can.

Jane I do not wish to annoy Mr Rochester, but ... please Mrs Fairfax, such a gathering I find quite frightening.

Mrs Fairfax I understand, my dear. I'll speak to Mr Rochester. Oh, I shall be glad when the party leaves. There are so many difficulties with the staff — and when the house has not been opened up for years — all the best rooms are in use, you know.

Jane Yes, there is so much for you to do.

Mrs Fairfax Cook is not used to preparing meals for such a number.

Jane Tell me, why does Mrs Poole not help on such occasions? Her work with the linen cannot demand so many hours.

Mrs Fairfax I — I don't think the master would consider that a practicality.

Jane But would you, Mrs Fairfax? Or do you think perhaps that her character and personality constrict her for such tasks?

Act I, Scene 4

Mrs Fairfax She is a strange woman, I'll admit. I fear that on occasion she drinks.
Jane But why then does she stay in service? It puzzles me.
Mrs Fairfax She has been here since the master returned from the West Indies, and he is happy with her work. We cannot question his opinion.
Jane No, of course not.
Mrs Fairfax Well, I must see if dinner is cleared. (*She crosses to the door*)
Jane Mrs Fairfax — you will not forget — to speak with Mr Rochester?
Mrs Fairfax No, I will not, my dear. (*In the doorway*) Jane, is everything all right? You are not unwell, are you?
Jane Why, of course not! Why do you ask?
Mrs Fairfax It is merely that you have been quiet of late. You are not unhappy here, are you, Jane?
Jane Why, no — I am most happy here. I have come to look on Thornfield as my home.
Mrs Fairfax I am glad, my dear, for this can be your home for many years to come. The master is most pleased with your work with Adèle. He has told me so several times.
Jane (*impulsively*) Does he like me, Mrs Fairfax?
Mrs Fairfax Like you, child? Why, whatever do you mean?
Jane I — well — I wondered if he disliked me or not. His manner is often quite odd when we meet.
Mrs Fairfax My dear, you should know the master better by this time. He is a deep man and does not readily show his inner feelings. His dislikes he will make most plain, but there is seldom an expression of delight.
Jane Yes — yes — I know. It was a stupid question. I — I don't know why I thought to ask.
Mrs Fairfax (*gently, eyeing her slowly*) We are all here to serve the household, you know, my dear, and we must not let our private thoughts interfere with our duty.
Jane I am well aware of that, Mrs Fairfax. Please do not misunderstand me.
Mrs Fairfax Then all is well. I must go down, my dear.

Mrs Fairfax exits

Jane wanders to the window where she sits gazing into the garden below. She casually fingers the curtains and thoroughly inspects the alcove before returning her eyes to the scene outside

John appears in the doorway

John Excuse me, miss. I've been told to fetch the brandy.

Jane That's all right, John — please do so.
John (*crosing to the cupboard and opening it*) We've always kept some up here for when the master used this room.

Jane continues gazing out of the window. John is about to exit

I hope I didn't disturb you, miss?
Jane No, of course not, John. I was just looking from the window. It is a fine night: the garden is lovely in this light.
John Well, be careful, miss. That window swings right out and it'd be a nasty fall.
Jane Yes, it would. When I was very young we had just such a window at the place where I lived — just such a window seat too. I used to sit for hours with my feet up here on the seat — and I'd pull the curtains about me so that no-one would know I was there. A little world of my own. It is useful to have such a retreat at times.
John Yes, miss.
Jane I'm sorry. Do not let me keep you, John.
John Thank you, miss.

John exits

Jane rises and restlessly crosses from the window. She picks up her cloak and is about to exit into her room

Rochester appears in the doorway UC

Rochester Miss Eyre. I understand you see fit to spurn my company this evening. I am most upset.
Jane (*turning, startled*) I — Mr Rochester — I apologize for not accepting your invitation, but — I have a headache, and — I thought my presence would not be conducive to the party atmosphere.
Rochester Oh — it is a party atmosphere, is it? You surprise me. I had not realized this: but I am desolated at the news of your ailment.
Jane (*sensing the sarcasm, but ignoring it*) I am grateful for your sympathy, sir.
Rochester Yes, I am astounded, too, at its rapidly changing symptoms.
Jane Sir?
Rochester A moment ago I was informed that you suffered from an upset of the stomach — something you had eaten.
Jane (*confused*) Well — yes, sir — that too.
Rochester But the headache is now prevalent? Is that so?
Jane Yes, sir.

Act I, Scene 4

Rochester Well, we must take care, young lady, lest a fever or the palsy be imminent!

Jane smiles in spite of herself

Oh, come now, Jane. You have not the talent of the deceiver, and your accomplices are lacking in any powers of the imagination. You are not ill — a little depressed perhaps — and pale as always, but not ill, are you?
Jane No, sir.
Rochester Just reluctant to meet this unfortunate visage in any avoidable circumstances?
Jane Oh no, sir. That is not true.
Rochester But yes. We have barely met these last weeks, hardly spoken since — since you half-drowned me.
Jane You have been gone for much of that time, sir.
Rochester Yes, that is true, but now — now I am back and for some little time.
Jane I am pleased to hear that, sir.
Rochester Are you? Well, I must tell you that while I am here, I am oft desirous of your company.
Jane But, sir, you have much company present in the house.
Rochester There are a number of people, Jane — some of whom are idiots and most of whom are bores. I have a duty to perform — a long neglected duty — to welcome local gentry and run the social gauntlet. It is something I do not take pleasure in.
Jane Is there not some other purpose in entertaining thus?
Rochester What's this? A question at last?
Jane Forgive me, sir — I had no right to ——
Rochester Nonsense, Jane. I give you leave to question me from time to time. I do not, however, promise to reply.
Jane You honour me, sir. I am but your humble servant.
Rochester You are much more than that, Jane. I owe you a great debt — one which I can never repay. And you are indeed a most noble creditor, for there is never a question asked — not a quizzical expression and this intrigues me. It is not in your nature to accept blindly. You are a creature of strength of spirit. Why do you not attack me? Demand reasons and explanations? Anyone would — this is not you, Jane.
Jane I fear that such demands, no matter how justly made, would be useless, sir.
Rochester Useless? How can you know? Am I so unapproachable?
Jane No, sir, but I am sure that if you could readily explain the strange events that occur in this house, then you would do so. I can only conclude that explanation is impossible and I must accept this.

Rochester Jane, never was there a woman of such understanding. And yet you are still a child.
Jane Not a child, sir.
Rochester But almost. And you are right. There is a secret here in this house and, as you have seen, a danger to me. But the secret must remain a secret and the danger must reside.
Blanche (*off*) Edward! Edward, where are you? Edward!
Rochester (*moving to the passageway*) Excuse me.

Blanche appears in the passageway

Blanche Oh, there you are, Edward. I've looked all over for you — everywhere. You've been trying to escape the party. (*She looks around the room, apparently not noticing Jane*) What a quaint room; what a hideaway.
Rochester It is a library doing service as a school-room.
Blanche Ah, but you use it as a secret place, a retreat, and we cannot allow that.
Rochester Forgive me. I had not meant to neglect my guests.
Blanche You were trying to escape the charades, but we have all been waiting for you. Henry and Frederick have been preparing everything. Oh, you must come at once.
Rochester Very well, Miss Ingram, but you must excuse me from the charades.
Blanche Oh, no. You must join in. There are no excuses. You will have such fun.
Rochester I very much doubt it. Are you fond of charades, Miss Eyre?
Blanche Oh, pardon me, I thought you were alone.
Rochester Miss Eyre, this is Miss Ingram — my dear, this is Jane Eyre, the governess to my ward Adèle.
Jane How do you do, ma'am.
Blanche I see — the governess. Oh, yes, Adèle — such a sweet child and you are so good to her, Edward.
Rochester I provide food and sustenance and a roof above her head — nothing more.
Blanche Yes, but you have such patience with her, Edward. I do admire those who can deal with the ways of children.
Rochester Then you must admire Miss Eyre, for she is the one who trains and guides her every minute of the day. I barely ever see the child.
Blanche Mm — well, of course, she is paid for it, is that not so?
Jane Yes, ma'am, that is so.
Blanche Edward, do come along now: the others are impatient.
Rochester Very well, we will go down. Miss Eyre, are you sure that you are not sufficiently recovered to join us in the charades?

Act I, Scene 4

Jane You are very kind, sir, but I would prefer not.
Blanche Edward, what a strange idea! Miss Eyre could hardly join the party.
Rochester And why not, pray?
Blanche Well, really Edward, what are you thinking of! Have you invited the kitchen maids as well?
Rochester No, Miss Ingram, I have not, as yet. Miss Eyre, however, is not a common kitchen maid, but a young woman of many gifts and of great intelligence, unlike a number of my guests downstairs.
Jane Sir, I beg of you — I am most concerned at this turn of conversation. Please may I be excused?
Rochester Nonsense, Miss Eyre.
Blanche Really, Edward, I must protest. Miss Eyre's presence in the drawing-room would be regarded, by my family at least, as a positive slight. You have upset me most profoundly.
Rochester My dear, you are too easily upset, but I apologize nevertheless. You are my guest in this house and I shall conform to your wishes. The drawing-room is barred to you, Miss Eyre. You must not set one foot inside the door for fear of driving the company into a frenzy!
Blanche Really, Edward!

Mrs Fairfax enters

Mrs Fairfax Excuse me, sir, but a gentleman has called. He apologizes for his inopportune arrival, but says he has been travelling many miles.
Rochester What is his business?
Mrs Fairfax He insists on seeing you, sir.
Rochester Well, what is his name, woman? Doesn't he send a card?
Mrs Fairfax (*handing a visiting card*) It is Mason, sir — Mr Mason.
Rochester (*quietly*) Mason, the devil it is.
Mrs Fairfax Shall I show him up, sir?
Rochester Where is he now, Mrs Fairfax?
Mrs Fairfax He just waits in the hall, sir. I did not know ——
Rochester All right, Mrs Fairfax, show him here.

Mrs Fairfax exits

Miss Ingram, you will have to excuse me, I must see this man. If you return to the drawing-room I shall join you as soon as possible.
Blanche Oh really, Edward. Why can't you send him away — see him tomorrow?
Rochester That is impossible, I assure you. I have no choice: I must see him now.
Blanche But what is all the mystery about?

Rochester Please do not concern yourself. I shall see him but briefly and come straight away.
Blanche Oh, very well, but you do neglect me, Edward. (*Stopping at the door*) Good-night, Miss Eyre.
Jane Good-night, ma'am.

Blanche exits

I shall retire, sir, if you wish to interview Mr Mason here.
Rochester Yes, Jane, I fear you must, though the prospect of this meeting is far from happy.
Jane Is there anything that I can do, sir. Can I help you in any way?
Rochester No, Jane, not now. But should occasion arise I would not hesitate to ask for your assistance.

Mrs Fairfax enters followed by Mr Mason, a man of medium height, heavily tanned, but with a weakness of face

Mrs Fairfax Mr Mason, sir.
Mason Edward — I — I'm very glad to see you.
Rochester Good-evening, Mason. It has been a long time.
Mason Yes, very long. Please excuse my sudden arrival. I — I wanted to warn you of my visit, but I came straightway from Liverpool.
Rochester Yes, yes. Sit down, man. Miss Eyre ... this is my ward's governess, Mason ... I apologize for supplanting you in your own sitting-room. You must forgive me, but it is necessary.
Jane I do understand, sir. I will leave you. Good-night, gentlemen.
Mason
Rochester } (*together*) Good-night.

Jane exits

Mason Can we be overheard?
Rochester No. And no one should disturb us, but dammit man, you arrive in the middle of a house party. What are my guests to think?
Mason I am most sorry, Edward, but father sent me and told me to make great haste. Forgive me. I am tired — the voyage has been dreadful, and now the day's travelling ...
Rochester You have not deserted the hot sun of the West Indies only to arrive with vivid descriptions of the hardships of travel, Mason. What brings you here?
Mason Give me time. I ——
Rochester No. You burst into my house and expect to be treated as a

welcome guest. Well, you are not welcome, Mason. Neither you nor the rest of your family.

Mason You are unjust, Edward. I have never harmed you.

Rochester You and your family have done me nothing but harm — ay, together with my own father. It was a thorough conspiracy, I'll admit, but jointly or individually you have all brought an everlasting grief into my life, a constant torment for which there is no answer this side of the grave.

Mason I was not responsible ——

Rochester Mason, state your business and leave my house. I have no wish to entertain you any longer than is necessary.

Slight pause

Mason So be it, Edward. The facts of the matter are that my father is dying — he may by now be deceased, for I have been travelling for many days. But his last wish was that I should discover the whereabouts of Bertha and then return and report as to her welfare.

Rochester So now he inquires — now he becomes concerned. The pangs of conscience strike, do they? Well, it is far too late, Mason. He will have to meet his maker without the peace of mind he so desires. I shall not help him.

Mason But he is dying — Edward, have compassion.

Rochester Who are you to speak of compassion? You, the pitiful messenger of an unholy strain. Neither you nor your father have ever shown me any such consideration. You sent me to my fate without a single gesture, a single word of warning.

Mason But we repent: I sincerely repent, Edward. And my father lives his last hours with this shadow on his life, longing for your forgiveness. You have admitted it was conspiracy that led you to the sorry state — a conspiracy only made possible by your father. There is the greater sin, surely — that he could — do this thing to you ——

Rochester You have no need to say these things. I am reminded every day of my father's callousness: his total disregard. This is his house and everywhere I see him — his grasping avaricious shadow lingers in every corner. I do not forget.

Mason Then help me, Edward; think better of my own father. He, perhaps, was led by stronger forces and by sheer despair. Tell me, where is she? Where is she kept?

A pause

Rochester What if I were to tell you she was dead and had been so these many years.

Mason Dead? But, Edward, is it true? Is it possible?
Rochester Quite possible.
Mason But how — where did she die? Under what circumstances?
Rochester She died here in this house immediately after our return to England.
Mason But how? What struck her down?
Rochester Nothing struck her down, Mason. She never lived for no-one knew of her presence.
Mason What! I do not understand.
Rochester No-one knew of her previous existence. My father had seen to that, and now no-one knows she is here.
Mason Here? Then she lives? She did not die?
Rochester Oh, yes. There is but a pale human form, held secret in this house. She is only human in appearance. To me she is dead.
Mason But, Edward — how can you ... what do people ... ?
Rochester She is cared for. She is fed and clothed and better her fate here than in one of the institutions for her kind. What I have told you is for your ears only — yours and your father's. Not one word of this must be breathed to another living soul or you will live to regret it. Do you understand?
Mason Of course I understand, Edward.
Rochester This discussion is at an end, Mason ... You must leave as soon as arrangements can be made.
Mason But — I must at least see her before I leave. This you must grant me.
Rochester I do not advise it, Mason. I think it both dangerous and useless.
Mason But I must, for my father's sake, I must. Why should it be dangerous?
Rochester She is a most dangerous animal, given at times to commit the most vicious crimes. I say it is useless, for I am quite sure she would not know you.
Mason Not know me? Then she is so much worse?
Rochester No, Mason, I have told you. She is dead and that is the only way in which I can think of her.
Mason It is quite horrible.
Rochester I will provide you with shelter for this night on condition that you go straight to your chamber without a word to the servants and leave as early as possible in the morning. (*He rings the bell*)
Mason That is good of you.
Rochester Do you agree to the conditions?
Mason Yes, yes I do.
Rochester Then I will put you in the hands of Mrs Fairfax, my housekeeper. I have guests I am sadly neglecting.
Mason I am sorry, Edward, but I could not delay.
Rochester Do not delay your departure, that is all I ask.

Act I, Scene 5

Mason I will not. (*After a pause*) Edward, should I return in time to speak with my father, is there some word ——
Rochester I cannot forgive, Mason.
Mason Will you send a man to the grave without ... ?
Rochester I have done what I can. It must suffice.

Mrs Fairfax enters

Mrs Fairfax You rang, sir?
Rochester Yes, Mrs Fairfax. Will you make ready one of the spare rooms for Mr Mason. He is staying overnight.
Mrs Fairfax Of course, sir.
Rochester And if Mr Mason should require anything, I would be grateful if you, yourself, would attend to his needs.
Mrs Fairfax Very well, sir.

Mrs Fairfax exits

Mason I am not in the habit of gossiping with maids, Edward; you need have no fear.
Rochester (*in the doorway, automatically looking up the stairs*) In this house there is always fear.
Mason Is — is that where she is? Up there?
Rochester Yes. Pray God we have a peaceful night.

They both exit

Fade to Black-out

Bright music for scene change

Scene 5

The same. Several hours later

The music fades and we hear the wind rising as the flicker of the fire is seen once more and moonlight through chinks in the curtains. The wind rises to a crescendo and is topped by a piercing scream and shouts are heard off R. *Then the maniacal laugh and running of feet before we distinguish Rochester's voice*

Rochester (*off*) Get out, man — get out!

Mason (*off*) Help — I can't — I can't!
Rochester (*off*) Be quick. I can't hold her. Get out.
Mason (*off, hysterically*) I'm hurt, Rochester. I'm hurt. Help me.
Rochester (*off*) Get on to the stairs!

A last wild scream of laughter and we hear a door slam and the running of feet descending the stairs

The double doors are thrown open and the light from the fire augmented by a passage light allows us to see the body of Mason lying at the foot of the stairs. He is dressed fully but we see blood issuing profusely from his neck. Rochester strides across to Jane's door and knocks urgently

Miss Eyre! Miss Eyre! Are you awake?
Jane (*off*) I'm coming, sir.
Rochester (*crossing back to Mason*) Be quick, girl. Mason — here — take my arm.

Jane enters

Jane I was up, sir. I heard the noise — what is ...?
Rochester Quickly, Jane, that chair. Mr Mason is hurt.
Mason (*groaning with the effort of moving*) Oh, God! Dear, God, I'm done for.
Rochester Quickly, Jane. Get water and a towel.

Jane exits to her room

Rochester eases away Mason's shirt

Mason Leave me be, Edward — I am finished.
Rochester Nonsense, man. It is nothing.
Mason I am in agony — look, the blood!
Rochester All right, Mason. It is not serious. Jane, be quick.
Mason She's an animal. You were right, Edward. It is horrible.
Rochester Be quiet. Don't talk.
Mason How could she do it — she was raving.
Rochester Silence, and lie still. Jane!

Jane enters with water and a towel

Jane Here, sir ...
Rochester Now be still, Mason. This will not hurt. We must stop the bleeding.

Act I, Scene 5 39

Mason Oh, there is such pain.
Rochester Jane, are you upset by the sight of blood?
Jane No, sir. Let me.
Rochester Quickly, hold the towel firm upon the wound. I will get bandages.

Rochester exits

Jane Hold still, sir. Let me help you ...
Mason I fear it's too late. She's done for me — me of all people.
Jane Hush, sir. Don't exert yourself.
Mason Savaged me like a wild animal. I could not defend myself.
Jane You are safe now, sir — please try to relax. You will be well, sir.
Mason Rochester! Rochester! Where is he? Rochester!

Rochester enters

Rochester Quiet, man. You'll have the entire household up here.
Mason Listen to me, Rochester. That woman — she ——
Rochester Not a word, man. Jane, bring that candle closer. What's that, salts?
Jane Yes, I brought them.
Rochester Good — give them to him while I bandage.
Mason Oh, it hurts, Rochester.
Rochester Yes, but it is not serious. If we can halt the flow of blood all will be well until you get to a surgeon. There is a very good man nearby.
Mason *(pushing the salts away)* She bit me, Rochester. She was like a tigress.
Rochester I know — I know.
Mason Thank God you got the knife away from her. Oh! it was terrible. I did not expect it, she looked so quiet at first.
Rochester I warned you. I told you not to see her.
Mason But I had to — for my father's sake. I thought I could have done some good.
Rochester You thought stupidly and now you have paid for it.
Mason She said she'd drain my heart.
Rochester Never mind her gibberish.
Mason I wish I could forget.
Rochester You will — you will.
Mason ... impossible to forget ...
Rochester Quiet ... Jane, go to my room and open the centre drawer of my table. There you will find a small phial. Bring it to me quickly.

Jane exits

Mason Oh, God, Rochester. I'd no idea she was so bad.

Rochester Do not talk so in front of Miss Eyre. She does not know my secret.
Mason What of this surgeon?
Rochester He will be discreet. He is the only other one I have taken into my confidence.

Jane enters with the phial

Jane The phial, sir.
Rochester Good. Jane, run to the stables and awaken the coachman there. Tell him Mr Mason is leaving and needs his coach at once, but that he must be most silent and not disturb the household.
Jane Yes, sir.

Jane exits

Rochester Now, Richard, drink this. It will give you the strength that you are lacking.
Mason God knows I need some strength. Tonight has been such horror I can never forget.
Rochester Tonight has been but one night. Now you know what life has been for me these many years.
Mason You are brave, Edward. I do not envy you your life.
Rochester I do not want your sympathy. I only look forward to your departure.
Mason Is there nothing I can do?
Rochester You have done enough in coming here. There is little time to waste. Are you strong enough to stand?
Mason With some assistance. I feel much better now.
Rochester Good — then lean on me.

Mason rises and is supported to the door

Easy — this way.
Mason Thank you. (*Pausing in the doorway*) Edward, let her be taken care of. Let her be treated as tenderly as may be.
Rochester I have done my best in the past and shall continue to do so. Yes, yet I would to God there was an end to it.

Jane appears in the doorway

Jane All is ready, sir.
Rochester Good. I shall be but a little while, Jane.

Act I, Scene 5

Mason and Rochester exit to L

Jane closes the doors, leaning on them with some relief, then she quickly crosses to the window and pulls open the curtains, revealing the early rays of the sun. She crosses and clears the bandages before returning to the window. We hear the distant clatter of horse and carriage retreating. She stands watching for a moment

The door is quietly opened by Rochester who gazes on her intently before speaking

You watch the sunrise, Jane?

She turns and he crosses to join her at the window

That sky with its high, light clouds which are sure to melt away as the day waxes warm.
Jane They are melting fast.
Rochester Yes. It is strange how the first light of day can either bewilder and depress or provide welcome relief from the dreams of the night.
Jane You find relief in this morning light, sir?
Rochester Yes, I do, Jane. We have passed a very strange night. It has made you look pale — have you been afraid?
Jane No, sir — only perhaps for a moment.
Rochester You have been magnificent.
Jane Sir, I must ask you, will Grace Poole still live here?
Rochester Yes, Jane, she will.
Jane But, sir, surely ...
Rochester Jane, you have never questioned me before. I beg of you, do not question me now. I know you think her guilty of these many strange events, but there is reason for her presence — good reason. Will you accept this?
Jane I have a trust in you, sir. You must do what you think fit.
Rochester Jane, your understanding is supreme.
Jane I would not be sure of that, sir.
Rochester But yes. Jane, call fancy to your aid and tell me — suppose that you, at a tender age, were to commit a grave error — not a crime, mark you — but error, and that in time the results of what you have done become utterly insupportable — you take measures to obtain relief, every measure that is neither culpable nor unlawful, but still you are miserable and hope has deserted you. Then suppose that after many years you meet a stranger and in this stranger you find a society that refreshes and regenerates your faith and hope for happiness. Is the wandering, repentant man justified in daring the world's opinion — in overleaping an obstacle of custom in order to attach himself forever to this gentle, gracious stranger?

Jane Sir, I am not qualified for such discussion. I would think that one who suffered in the way that you describe should look higher than his equal for strength and solace.

Rochester But the instrument! God ordains the instrument, and if I — if such a man finds the instrument for cure before him, should not he ignore the worldly customs to find his salvation?

A slight pause

Jane Does such a man always recognize the correct instrument? Is he not easily confused and persuaded to the wrong course?

Rochester No, Jane. When a man has searched for so long without success, he is seldom mistaken when the object of his desire at last appears.

Jane Then if there is such conviction there is only one answer.

Rochester Do you really believe that, Jane? Do you?

Jane I do, sir — but it grieves me that it be so.

Rochester But why? Why should it?

Jane For a purely selfish reason, Mr Rochester.

Rochester But tell me — what?

Jane I grieve to leave Thornfield: I love Thornfield: I love it, because I have lived in it a full and delightful life — momentarily at least. I have not been trampled on. I have not been petrified. I have not been buried with inferior minds, and excluded from every glimpse of communion with what is bright and energetic and high. I have talked, face to face, with what I revere, with what I delight in — with an original, a vigorous, an expanded mind. I have known you Mr Rochester; and it strikes me with terror and anguish to feel I absolutely must be torn from you for ever. I see the necessity of departure; and it is like looking at the necessity of death.

Rochester Where, where do you see the necessity?

Jane You sir, have placed it before me.

Rochester But no — I certainly have not.

Jane You have, sir — truly you have. You would take a bride — that is the subject of your question. You are to marry ...

Rochester It is — yes, Jane, I am to marry ...

Jane Then I tell you I must go! Do you think I can stay to become nothing to you? Do you think I am an automaton? — a machine without feelings? — and can bear to have my morsel of bread snatched from my lips and my drop of living water dashed from my cup? Do you think because I am poor, obscure, plain and little, I am soulless and heartless? You think wrong! I have as much soul as you — and full as much heart. And if God had gifted me with some beauty and some wealth, I should have made it awkward for you to leave me, as it is now for me to leave you. I am not speaking to you

Act I, Scene 5   43

    now through the medium of custom, conventionalities nor even mortal
    flesh: it is my spirit that addresses your spirit; just as if we both had passed
    through the grave, and we stood at God's feet, equal — as we are!
Rochester As we are! So Jane!
Jane Yes, so sir! And yet not so! For you are a married man — or as good
    as a married man and wed to one with whom you have no sympathy —
    whom I do not believe you truly love, one inferior to you.
Rochester She is never that.
Jane She has position ...
Rochester A plain, pale creature — noble, perhaps ...
Jane Sir — Miss Ingram certainly ...
Rochester *Miss Ingram?* Jane, you have never been so stupid!
Jane Sir, what do you ... ?
Rochester I summon you as my wife. (*Shouting*) You, Jane!

She does not answer

    (*Gently*) Jane, do you doubt me?
Jane (*weakly*) Entirely.
Rochester You have no faith in me?
Jane Not a whit.
Rochester You little sceptic — you shall be convinced. What love have I for
    Miss Ingram? None — and you should know that.
Jane But you seemed to be together ...
Rochester Her father drives her to me: he longs for my estates ...
Jane But she surely loves you.
Rochester That creature only loves herself. But what is this talk of her? Jane
    — you — you I love. I entreat you, accept me as a husband.
Jane I cannot believe you are in earnest. Do you sincerely want me for your
    wife?
Rochester I do. And if an oath is necessary — I swear it.
Jane Then, sir — I will, oh! I will marry you.
Rochester Jane! Oh, Jane.

They embrace

    What happiness you give me with these simple words, Jane ——

They kiss

Jane Sir, if I ever did a good deed in my life, if I ever thought a good thought,
    if I ever prayed a sincere and blameless prayer, if I ever wished a righteous
    wish, to be your wife is for me to be as happy as I can be on earth.

Rochester You love me, Jane?
Jane With all my heart I do. A poor governess and you ...
Rochester Then have no fear. God pardon me! And man not meddle with me! I have her and I will hold her.

They kiss, as ——

—— the CURTAIN *falls*

ACT II

Scene 1

The same. July, 1847

The Curtain *rises to reveal the library in some disorder. The furniture has been cleared from* c *and a trunk stands open in its place. The double doors are open through which we can see Rochester's apartment also open*

Leah is hurriedly packing clothes into the trunk, having completed packing Jane's box with which she arrived. Adèle is skipping excitedly about

Leah Be still, Miss Adèle: I can't see what I'm doing.
Adèle Oh, Leah, it is so exciting the marriage of M'sieur Rochester. I am so 'appy about it — so glad it is Miss Aire.
Leah They may get married this morning, but they certainly won't be able to leave today if I don't get this trunk packed.

Adèle is holding a dress against her and twirling round

  Miss Adèle, stop that.
Mrs Fairfax (*off*) Leah! Leah — have you finished the trunk?
Leah (*calling*) Not yet, ma'am. (*To herself*) I don't know how she expects ——

Mrs Fairfax appears in Rochester's doorway

Mrs Fairfax Well, do be sure you've packed the linen in Miss Eyre's room. It is on the chest. (*She comes into the library*)
Leah Yes, ma'am.
Adèle Where is M'sieur Rochester? Why is he not 'ere?
Mrs Fairfax He is dressing in the other wing, Adèle, so that Miss Eyre can use his apartment for her preparations.
Adèle Can I see her, madam? Can I see her?
Mrs Fairfax She is not ready yet, Adèle.
Adèle When, please? When can I see her in the wedding dress?
Mrs Fairfax Just be patient, Adèle.

Leah Has Miss Eyre got all her travelling clothes in there, ma'am?
Mrs Fairfax Yes, she has everything. Pack all that is left in her room, then John can take down the luggage. Mr Rochester wishes to leave immediately after the service, you know.
Leah Yes, ma'am.

Leah exits to Jane's room

Mrs Fairfax Now, Adèle, you must go and dress. Run and tell Sophie to help you.
Adèle Ooh, I want to see Miss Aire: please let me see 'er in the dress.
Mrs Fairfax You must wait and see her in the church.

John enters

John I've taken Mr Rochester's luggage to the carriage, ma'am. Is Miss Eyre's ready yet?
Mrs Fairfax Not quite, John, but don't go away. Leah! Leah!

Leah enters

Leah Here, ma'am.
Mrs Fairfax Do be quick, Leah. It is nearly time to leave. I must go back to Jane. Now hurry or you won't be ready yourselves. (*Taking hold of Adèle*) Now run along, Adèle, and do as I tell you.
Adèle (*in the passageway*) But, madame ...
Mrs Fairfax No — no, quickly.

Adèle exits downstairs and Mrs Fairfax goes into Rochester's room

Leah I've got a fine chance to get ready! Why is there such a rush for them to be off, that's what I'd like to know.
John I don't know, I'm sure. I thought they weren't going 'til tomorrow.
Leah I shan't be ready in time to get to the church, I know I won't — and me with a new bonnet to wear.
John Can I take this box down?
Leah Yes, and I should smarten yourself up if I were you.
John What do you mean?
Leah Well, going to a wedding like that!
John Well, I've got me clean waistcoat on, an' me necktie. What more d'you want?
Leah I want you to sit on this trunk while I strap it.
John 'Ere, I'll do it.

Act II, Scene 1   47

Leah I should think so. Ooh, no — there's another dress. Wait. (*Crossing to Jane's room*) Take the other box while I fetch it.

Leah exits

John (*surveying the scene*) Lot more luggage than when she came.
Leah (*off*) Well, there's lots of fine things the master's bought 'er these last weeks.
John (*picking up the box*) I'll take this down then.

Leah enters with the dress

Leah Come straight back then for the trunk.

Mrs Fairfax enters

Mrs Fairfax Oh, John — good. You're taking the things down. Leah, are you ready?

John exits with the box

Leah Just finished, ma'am.
Mrs Fairfax Now you know your place in the church Leah, don't you?
Leah Yes, ma'am.
Mrs Fairfax And be sure that Sophie and the other maids behave themselves.
Leah I'll try, ma'am. Is Miss Eyre ready now, ma'am?
Mrs Fairfax Very nearly. Now there's just this trunk. Oh, what time is it?
Leah Nearly twelve by the clock, ma'am.
Mrs Fairfax I wonder if Mr Rochester is ready?
Rochester (*off* R) Mrs Fairfax — Mrs Fairfax — where are you?
Mrs Fairfax Oh, dear — I'm in here, Mr Rochester.

Rochester enters

Rochester It is time, Mrs Fairfax. Is all prepared?
Mrs Fairfax Very nearly, sir. Run along, Leah.
Leah Yes, ma'am.

Leah exits

Rochester Where is Jane — Miss Eyre? Is she ready?
Mrs Fairfax Yes, sir.

Rochester Then bring her to me.
Mrs Fairfax (*shocked*) Oh, but sir, I ...
Rochester What is it? Is something wrong?
Mrs Fairfax But, sir, you must not see her.
Rochester Why ever not, woman?
Mrs Fairfax If the groom sees the bride before the wedding, sir, it means dreadful bad luck.
Rochester Nonsense, woman. We have but a short walk to the church beyond the gates, but I would fain make the journey unaccompanied. Quick, make haste, Mr Wood will be putting on his surplice. Tell Jane I would speak with her.
Mrs Fairfax Very well, sir.

John enters as Mrs Fairfax exits

Rochester Ah, John, is the carriage made ready?
John Yes, sir, but for this trunk.
Rochester Good, we shall not want it for the church, but it must be ready the moment we return — be quick, man.
John Yes, sir. (*He takes the trunk to the door and pauses*) Er — sir ...
Rochester Yes?
John May I wish you all the luck, sir?
Rochester Thank you, John, thank you.
John Sir.

John exits, closing the door behind him

Rochester turns, facing the window

After a moment the door opens and Jane appears in full bridal costume

Rochester stares wonderingly at her for a long second

Rochester Jane, Jane, what have you done? What mischief are you at to make you appear so?
Jane Forgive me, but I do not understand.
Rochester You look as fair as a lily; not only the pride of my life but the desire of my eyes. Is this my plain little elf?
Jane Edward, you are wicked to make such fun of me.
Rochester No, no, I am not wicked and I do not make fun. I am true and just. Look hard into the glass and you will see how your complexion has ripened; your eyes become brighter; your lips fresh and as sweet as a new rose.

Act II, Scene 1

Jane If you speak truth, sir, then I can only answer that it is you that wrought these changes. It is happiness that brightens my eye and alters my complexion — happiness found in you, Edward.

Rochester *(taking out a jewel case)* For you, Jane, the heirlooms for the lady of Thornfield.

Jane Oh Edward, it is beautiful — but please not jewels. Jewels for Jane Eyre are unnatural and strange — I would rather not have them.

Rochester But a present you must have on such a day ...

Jane Please sir, truly I would rather not have it. If I wear it, you will not know me — indeed I would not know myself and I would no longer be your Jane Eyre.

Rochester It is rich to see and hear you, Jane, and you are indeed original. I would not have you any other way. I love you more than I have ever dreamed of loving anyone.

Jane And I love you, Edward, with all my heart.

They kiss

Rochester Come — come quickly — my brain is on fire with impatience.

Jane I am quite ready, Edward.

Rochester Are you, Jane? Are you ready for the many years ahead, for the future we will share?

Jane Yes, Edward, I am.

Rochester Then take my arm, Jane, and we will go together.

They are c and as the line is spoken, softly we hear the sound of organ music and they slowly walk downstage as the Lights dim around them, leaving only a pool of light into which they move. Simultaneously, a French flat is flown in behind them representing the church window and the black tabs L and R. The music rises

Reverend Wood enters downstage and comes to stand between them. Behind, we dimly see the figures of servants and of strangers congregating. Adèle is dressed as a bridesmaid, with posy, etc.

When all effects are completed the organ fades

Wood ... which holy estate Christ adorned and beautified with his presence, and first miracle that He wrought in Cana of Galilee. In which holy estate these two persons present come now to be joined. Therefore I require and charge you both, as ye will answer at the dreadful day of judgment when the secrets of all hearts shall be disclosed, that if either of you know any impediment why ye may not lawfully be joined together in matrimony, ye do now confess it. For be ye well assured, that so many as are coupled together otherwise than in God's word doth allow, are not joined together by God, neither is their matrimony lawful. (*After a pause*) Do you, Edward ...

Mason appears from the shadows

Mason The marriage cannot go on — I declare an impediment.
Rochester (*spinning round*) Mason!
Mason I ... I'm sorry, Edward. I could not ...
Rochester Be silent! Proceed, Reverend, proceed!
Wood I cannot proceed without some investigation: an impediment has been asserted.
Mason Yes, and justly so I fear.
Rochester Do not listen to this man. I demand that you continue.
Wood You have no right to make demand, sir. I have a duty to perform. (*To Mason*) Come forward, sir. Pray tell me what is the nature of the said impediment? Perhaps we can surmount this difficulty — is it perhaps misunderstanding?
Mason I heartily wish that it were, but there is no mistake. The impediment is insuperable.
Wood Then state it, sir, without delay.
Rochester Go to hell, Mason!
Wood Hush, sir — remember where you are.
Mason Edward, I deeply regret, but I must speak.
Rochester Have you not done enough?
Wood Speak, sir.
Mason Edward Rochester is already married!

There is a ripple of sensation throughout the church

Mason I have the paper. The woman is my sister. I saw her last April when I visited Thornfield. She is living there now.
Wood At Thornfield Hall? Impossible! I am an old resident in this neighbourhood and I never heard of a Mrs Rochester at Thornfield Hall.
Mason It is true, sir. She is locked away and cared for by Grace Poole.

Sensation

Wood Can this be possible?
Rochester Yes, Reverend — it is quite possible.
Jane Edward!

Act II, Scene 1   51

Rochester Close your book, Reverend, and put away your surplice; there will be no wedding to-day. Bigamy is an ugly word. I meant, however, to be a bigamist. But fate has out-manœuvred me. To you I am little better than a devil at this moment. But you will hear me out. You say you have never heard of a Mrs Rochester at my house. I took great pains that you shouldn't — for her sake as well as mine. I now inform you that what you have heard is true. Bertha Mason is my wife; she is mad and comes from a mad family; maniacs and lunatics all of them, through three generations. He knew it; his father knew it; my father knew it. But they were all silent and sent me to my fate. Even you cannot possibly judge whether or not I had the right to break the contract and seek sympathy with something at least human. My wife is a wild, raging animal. Hers was the only conjugal embrace I was ever to know. And this is what I wished to have; this young girl who stands so grave and quiet. So I defy you to judge me now!

There is a buzz from the congregation

Wood This is incredible...
Mason It is true. There was a conspiracy of silence.
Jane (*softly*) Edward ...
Wood This is dreadful, quite dreadful!

Reverend Wood, Mason and the congregation slowly disperse into the shadows

Jane and Rochester are left in a pool of light

Rochester Jane, forgive me. Please tell me I have not destroyed your love.
Jane That could never happen, but we are lost.
Rochester No, not if we are together; happiness will be there. We can find another home, across the seas, away from all foul influence. Just stay by me, Jane.
Jane No, no, it is impossible. You have a wife. I must leave you now.
Rochester Jane, do you mean to go one way in this world and let me go another?
Jane I do.
Rochester Jane. (*He embraces her*) Do you mean it now?
Jane I do.
Rochester And now? (*He kisses her forehead and cheek*)
Jane I do.
Rochester Oh Jane, this is bitter! This is wicked. It would not be wicked to love me.

Jane It would be wicked to obey you.
Rochester Jane, give one glance to my horrible life when you are gone. All happiness torn away with you. What then is left? What shall I do? Where turn for a companion and some hope?
Jane Do as I do, trust in God and yourself. Believe in heaven and hope to meet there again.
Rochester Then you condemn me to live wretched and die accursed?
Jane I advise you to live sinless and I wish you to die tranquil.
Rochester Then you snatch love and innocence from me?
Jane Mr Rochester, I no more assign this fate to you than I would for myself.
Rochester Is it better to drive a fellow creature to despair than to transgress a mere human law?
Jane Laws and principles are not for times when there is no temptation; they are for moments such as this.
Rochester You are going, Jane? You are leaving me?
Jane I am going, sir.
Rochester You will not be my comforter, my rescuer? My deep love, my frantic prayers are all nothing to you? Jane, don't leave me here in anguish. Oh Jane! My hope — my love — my life!
Jane God bless you my dear master! God keep you from harm and wrong and reward you well for all your past kindness to me. It would be mortal sin to rest a moment longer.
Rochester No Jane, it is no sin to find a heaven.
Jane There is no hope of finding heaven now, we are destroyed.
Rochester But not our love.
Jane If I stay, it will wither and die...
Rochester I plead with you — do not desert me!
Jane (*moving into the shadows*) I must, dear Edward, I must!
Rochester You condemn me, Jane. You condemn me.....
Jane No I love! — I only love!

Jane goes

CURTAIN

SCENE 2

The Library. An evening in March, 1848

The CURTAIN *rises and we see the room in good order. The candles flicker as the wind howls outside. Rochester sits in the armchair above the fire gazing*

Act II, Scene 2

intently at the dancing flames. He holds a glass of brandy before him, but he does not drink

There is a long moment before Mrs Fairfax enters

Mrs Fairfax Good-evening, sir. (*She pauses but there is no answer*) I — I wondered if you would take something to eat, sir. It is getting quite late.
Rochester Mmm; no, Mrs Fairfax. I shall not dine this evening.
Mrs Fairfax But sir, you must have something. Just a light dish. You barely had a thing at luncheon.
Rochester No thank you, Mrs Fairfax. I have no appetite.
Mrs Fairfax Truly, sir, you will fall sick if this goes on. You have not eaten ——
Rochester (*angrily*) Stop fussing, woman. I wish to be left in peace — go away!
Mrs Fairfax (*after a moment*) Sir. (*She doesn't move*)
Rochester Mrs Fairfax.
Mrs Fairfax Sir?
Rochester Forgive me, my mood is most unpleasant — I apologize.
Mrs Fairfax There is no need, sir — I understand.
Rochester (*looking at her, almost fondly*) Hmm, yes, perhaps you do. (*He rises abruptly and walks to the window*) Perhaps you do.
Mrs Fairfax (*tentatively*) I have been a long time here at Thornfield, Mr Rochester.
Rochester Yes, yes, it has been many years. Many long years, but none so long as this last.
Mrs Fairfax Sir, may I say — these last months staying here you have seemed so low. There was a time when travel occupied the mind. Perhaps a visit to the continent would cheer you.
Rochester The continent — and what would I do there?
Mrs Fairfax Well, with Adèle now away at school, there is nothing to keep you here, sir. I just thought ...
Rochester Travel cannot console me now. I could search all the world and not find what I once had here in Thornfield.
Mrs Fairfax You must try to forget her, sir. She is gone.
Rochester Yes — gone, but where, where can she be? Why cannot I find trace of her? I was sure she would return to Lowood School. It was the obvious haven for her.
Mrs Fairfax Perhaps that was the reason she did not return there, sir.
Rochester Perhaps! She was most diligent in leaving no clue. She hides from me most carefully.
Mrs Fairfax She had to leave here, after — after the truth was revealed.

Rochester You think I did wrong? I know I did. I wanted her so desperately. It seemed ... and then that damned Mason.
Mrs Fairfax It was for the best, sir, you must see that. It was wrong to deceive her so.
Rochester Yes, yes — I know that now.
Mrs Fairfax Then you must start to live again, sir: try to forget the past. No good can come of that.
Rochester I cannot forget — I cannot ...
Mrs Fairfax But you must, sir. All this past year you have barely left this house for more than an hour. You have become a recluse — stifled your spirit; it is so bad for you.
Rochester I cannot leave, I dare not. You may not understand, Mrs Fairfax, but I — I hope one day she might return, and for this I must remain.
Mrs Fairfax It is a most slender hope, sir.
Rochester I know well enough, but it is hope.

Pause

Mrs Fairfax Well, I'll go down, sir. Do you want me to have the fire made up?
Rochester No, thank you, Mrs Fairfax — it is not necessary. There are still some logs.
Mrs Fairfax It is a bad night, sir. There is a storm coming, I think.
Rochester Yes, you are right. Mrs Fairfax — how is the patient?
Mrs Fairfax I do not know, sir. Mrs Poole has not been down since morning, sir.
Rochester I think perhaps I will see Mrs Poole. Would you send word?
Mrs Fairfax Yes, sir — I'll go at once.
Rochester Thank you.

Mrs Fairfax exits

Rochester pours more brandy and crosses to the cupboard. From it he takes Jane's portfolio. He opens it and examines the contents intently

Grace Poole enters

Mrs Poole You wanted me, sir?
Rochester How is the patient, Mrs Poole?
Mrs Poole As usual — always the same.
Rochester That is no answer, Mrs Poole. What state is she in at this moment? Does she rave or is she quiet?
Mrs Poole Oh, she's quiet, and sullen — the time I fear most.

Act II, Scene 2

Rochester Then you must be vigilant — take great care.
Mrs Poole Yes, sir. I will, sir.

Rochester moves restlessly towards the window

I will go back then, sir.

Pause. She moves to door

Rochester Mrs Poole.
Mrs Poole Sir?
Rochester It was you who informed Mr Mason of my intent to marry, wasn't it?
Mrs Poole Sir, I don't know what you speak of.
Rochester Yes, you do. You cannot hide it now. No-one else could have been responsible.
Mrs Poole No, sir — no.
Rochester Do not deny it. You sent word to Mason that a marriage was arranged ...
Mrs Poole I didn't — no, sir ...
Rochester Do not lie to me, woman. I am no fool. No other person knew she was my wife — no other person had the reason.
Mrs Poole Oh, sir — please.
Rochester You betrayed me — you pointed the finger.
Mrs Poole Oh, sir — forgive me, sir ...
Rochester Just report to me the facts. I want to know how it did come about.
Mrs Poole Oh, sir, I'm sorry. Please forgive me. I'll tell you, sir, only ...
Rochester Tell me the truth and do not be afraid. How did you know of Mason? The only time you saw him was the night he was attacked.
Mrs Poole I knew it was her brother for she spoke of him quite clearly after it was done. She knew who she'd attacked. She hated him, she said.
Rochester But where did you find him — how?
Mrs Poole He sent word to me, sir, while he was being nursed at the surgeon's house. He sent his coachman ...
Rochester Ah, the coachman! Then he bribed you, did he?
Mrs Poole No, sir — no. He was just concerned with her. He asked me to send word to a Mr Briggs in London.
Rochester Briggs? The solicitor?
Mrs Poole Yes, sir. He said, Mr Mason, that I was to let Mr Briggs know if there was any change in her or if she was removed to another place.
Rochester And he offered you rewards for any such information, did he not?
Mrs Poole Yes, yes he did, sir. But it wasn't that, sir. I did not want to do wrong, sir: that was all, sir ... (*She cries bitterly*)

Rochester Enough. I had hoped for greater loyalty, Grace Poole. I have paid you well for your unpleasant task.
Mrs Poole I know, sir — you have, sir ...
Rochester But I do not blame you now. I have only questioned you for one good reason. I thought perhaps you held the answer to where — but no — it is no use.
Mrs Poole I'm sorry, sir. I wish that I could make amends.
Rochester Then continue with your task and pray that its conclusion is not far away.
Mrs Poole Yes, sir.
Rochester You may go, Mrs Poole.
Mrs Poole Thank you, sir.

Mrs Poole exits

Rochester stands a moment, his hands to his brow. He seems to suffer from a great exhaustion. He sighs and automatically picks up the portfolio once more. Sitting again in the armchair he stares for a long moment at the topmost picture

Rochester (*softly*) Dear, sweet Jane — why did you never show me this? This strange self-likeness — passionately drawn. Here, you captured wholeheartedly your thought — not just the pale shadow as in your other works. But why this emotion? Why did you see yourself as such? These harsh lines do you ill. They turn the plain and honest feature to the harsh irregularity. You emphasize the unattractive. No ugliness was ever in you, Jane — and yet you felt an ugliness when painting here. But no matter — for you once said beauty was of little consequence and then I disagreed. But that was in a desperate, unknowing time and I was ignorant. Material beauty is of little consequence — I know that now; or you would never find a love for me ... But we did have a beauty, Jane — inside us and between us. It stretched from heart to heart like a web of silk. Our love was beauty ... Ooh, Jane ... Jane ... Jane ...

The Lights fade to Black-out

Scene 3

The same. Several hours later

The fire glows red in the grate. Suddenly there is a crash of thunder followed by the sound of rain and the flash of lightning. Rochester is slumped in the

Act II, Scene 3

armchair. The portfolio has fallen to the floor. There is the sound of running feet off stage

Mrs Poole (*off*) Help — help! Mr Rochester. Help — please.

The door bursts open and Mrs Poole stands there, distraught

Sir, Mr Rochester ...
Rochester (*springing up*) What is it, woman?
Mrs Poole (*choking*) Fire, sir! Fire upstairs! Please come, sir ...

Rochester crosses hurriedly to the main doors

Rochester Quickly, waken the house — get the servants.

He exits

Mrs Poole Sir, I could not help it: she — found the candle ...
Rochester (*off*) Don't talk, woman — get help.

John appears in the passageway R

John What is it? What's the noise?
Mrs Poole Fire — fire upstairs. She's set the room alight ...
Rochester (*off*) John — quickly, get water.

Mrs Fairfax enters from L

Mrs Fairfax What is it? Mrs Poole, what has happened?
John The maniac has set us afire, ma'am ...

John exits to Jane's room

Mrs Poole Water — we must get water. (*Opening Rochester's door*) We shall all be burnt alive ...
Rochester (*off*) Get help down there — bring the jugs ...
Mrs Fairfax Mr Rochester! Mr Rochester!

John enters with a jug of water. Rochester enters in the passageway. Leah enters

Mrs Fairfax Where is she, sir? Where is your wife?
Mrs Poole Still there, dancing in the flames. Oh, sir — I couldn't help it: I tried to stop her.

Rochester crosses into the library. Leah, Mrs Poole and Mrs Fairfax follow

Rochester Be quiet, Mrs Poole ... (*To Mrs Fairfax*) Get everybody down, Mrs Fairfax; take your things and get out of the house ... Get out! Get the women out!

Everyone exits

There is a flash of lightning followed by thunder. Smoke billows forth from the staircase

Rochester and Bertha appear from the stairs struggling. She carries a "burning" brand and wears a long white gown which is torn and dirtied; her long dark hair, a tangled mane

They descend to the passageway and Rochester falls. Bertha runs into the library

Rochester (*trying to grab her*) Hold still, you demon, hold still.
Bertha Fire — fire! I did it — the flames — I did it.
Rochester Stop struggling, or we are finished ... hold still.
Bertha Let go, let go! I'll kill you, kill you!

Bertha struggles free from him and attacks him with the brand

Burn — I want to burn: the flames — all burn — flames ...
Rochester Stop, stop!

She pushes him back and he screams as he falls. She stands above him, screaming with laughter

Bertha ... Bertha, no — stop, don't!
Bertha (*running around the library*) Fire — more flames — more flames.
Rochester (*clutching his face, he follows her and holds her* c) Don't! Don't! Stop, Bertha ...
Bertha Kill you — kill you! Burn — burn at the stake ...

She breaks away from him and flees to the window

Rochester Bertha — Bertha —— (*He goes towards her*)
Bertha Don't come near: I must not be touched. Keep away — keep away.
Rochester We must get out ...
Bertha Get back — away! Burn — burn. We must all burn ...

Act II, Scene 4

Rochester Be calm — stop — be calm ...
Bertha (*backing to the window seat*) No — no — fire ...
Rochester Must get out ...
Bertha The curtains!
Rochester The window! ... Bertha!

There is a terrible scream as she falls out and down and Rochester at the window collapses. A crash of thunder

CURTAIN

SCENE 4

The same. A few days later. Late afternoon

The CURTAIN *rises to reveal the library in some disorder. The passageway to the right of the double doors is boarded across and the room itself is robbed of much of its furniture. The windows are bare and the dismal afternoon light strikes harshly on the empty bookshelves*

Rochester is sitting in the wing armchair, his face concealed from view. The Reverend Wood is taking tea whilst intoning monotonously

Wood And it is difficult to understand at such times that there are sacrifices to be made. It is undeniable. It is of course a part of the great design, an important part. It is God's will, and we must be happy and accept the hardships.
Rochester Have some more tea, Wood.
Wood Er — well, yes, thank you. Would you care for a cup yourself now? It is quite warm still.
Rochester Forgive me if I decline.

There is an awkward pause

Wood You know, Mr Rochester, you look a good deal better today. I think your health improves.
Rochester I am well enough.
Wood What a remarkable escape you had, overcome by smoke and all. It was John, was it not, who rescued you.
Rochester Yes, it was John.
Wood And the fortunate storm to hold back the blaze — a miracle the whole house was not burnt. It is only the upper floor badly damaged, is it not?

Rochester (*wearily*) Only the upper floor — yes.
Wood Yes, from outside one can see that this side suffered most in the catastrophe. But finding you sitting here, I wondered ...
Rochester I sit here because I am most fond of this room.
Wood Yes — yes, it is a most pleasant room under other circumstances. And you intend to stay on here whilst all the repairs are made?
Rochester Naturally I will stay.
Wood I only wondered if perhaps you planned to go away ...
Rochester You need have no fear, Wood, there is no danger of your losing my patronage.
Wood Oh, but sir, that was most distant in my thoughts. My principal concern is for your welfare. You have had a most profound shock, a terrible experience, and I am here to render whatever services I may.
Rochester Yes — I do appreciate ...
Wood There are times, Mr Rochester, when even the strongest of men needs spiritual support and guidance and you have suffered such appalling loss just these few days ago. You must not hesitate to confide in me.
Rochester (*breaking in*) I can assure you, Reverend, that you need have little worry over me.
Wood But we must all care for one another, sir — as brother and sister of the great family.
Rochester Do you have the time, Reverend?
Wood Time? Er — yes. It is just thirty minutes after four o'clock.
Rochester Four — then it is time for my exercise.
Wood Yes, yes, of course — a wonderful thing, exercise. Perhaps I might even join you on your walk: we could continue our conversation.
Rochester Do you not have other duties, Wood?
Wood No, no; do not worry for that. I am in no hurry — I shall accompany you ...
Rochester (*springing to his feet*) No — that will not be necessary ... I — I ...

Rochester is now seen full face. He looks sickly pale. His eyes lie in great hollows and he bears a scar across his forehead. The effort of his sudden rise hits him and he clings, swaying a little, to the back of the chair

Wood Mr Rochester, are you all right?
Rochester Yes, yes — quite all right. You must excuse me.
Wood Yes, yes, of course. I will leave you then.
Rochester Kindly ring the bell.
Wood Certainly, certainly. Well, I will visit you again quite shortly ——
Rochester I'm sure you will!
Wood — and the next time I hope to find you even further recovered and in higher spirits.

Act II, Scene 4   61

Rochester I'm sure that you will.
Wood And do not despair, Mr Rochester. The Lord taketh away and he giveth. You will find happiness soon, I know it ——
Rochester You know, do you, Wood? Then you are a man of great vision.
Wood You must have faith, sir.
Rochester (*bitterly*) Faith! Faith in what?
Wood (*shocked*) Why, in the Lord, of course.
Rochester Hm! Yes — yes, of course, Reverend. Faith in the Lord.

Leah enters

Leah You rang, sir?
Rochester Show the Reverend out, Leah, and kindly ask Mrs Fairfax to come up. Good-evening, Wood. (*He holds out his hand, not moving*)
Wood (*going to Rochester and shaking hands*) Good-afternoon, Mr Rochester. God be with you.
Rochester Thank you. (*Firmly*) Good-afternoon.

Leah and Wood exit

Rochester turns and in doing so knocks the small table. He viciously lashes out at it and throws it over

Damnation! (*He crosses, supporting himself on furniture, to the window, where he stands, his gaze intent upon the sky-line*)

Mrs Fairfax enters. She has a small medicine glass

Mrs Fairfax I have brought your medicine.
Rochester Where have you been? You leave me here alone defenceless with that gibbering old fool.
Mrs Fairfax Sir, I thought it was your wish to be alone ... (*She picks up the table*)
Rochester Alone, yes — not coupled with that stupid man, or any other. I do not want intrusion, is that understood?
Mrs Fairfax Yes, sir, but you understand there are many who wish to call — to offer sympathy.
Rochester Pity? That is what they wish to serve — pity?
Mrs Fairfax You are upset, sir: do not excite yourself further. Come and sit down. (*She takes his arm*)
Rochester Let go my arm, woman! I am not crippled though you would have me so.
Mrs Fairfax You are not well, sir, and you must take care. Now please take this draught. The surgeon insists on its value.

Rochester Leave it there and I will take it.
Mrs Fairfax Please, sir, take it now.
Rochester Do as you are told, woman. You seem to think my disability gives you all the right to rule my life. Well, it does not!
Mrs Fairfax No, sir.

The excitement has tired him and he sways a little

Rochester The — the chair. Help me ...
Mrs Fairfax Sir — quickly here. (*She supports him to the armchair*) Oh dear, sir, you really must take care. Here now — rest.
Rochester I will — I will.
Mrs Fairfax (*handing him medicine*) Take this, sir.
Rochester What?
Mrs Fairfax Sir, I beg of you.
Rochester You will have your way, Mrs Fairfax.
Mrs Fairfax It is only the proper way, sir. Now — you sit awhile and I will come back to take you to the other wing. All the servants are busy putting it in order. Your new sleeping quarters are almost prepared.
Rochester I will be loath to leave this room: it has been sanctuary for me of late.
Mrs Fairfax You will soon be used to the other apartment. Now I must go about my work: shall I send John to sit with you?
Rochester No, I would prefer to be alone.
Mrs Fairfax Then rest awhile. I shall not be long away.
Rochester Do not trouble with me.

Mrs Fairfax turns and smiles at his back and then exits

Rochester, after a moment, gets up and moves up to the cupboard. From here he takes Jane's portfolio and without looking at it he crosses back and sits. He leans back, closing his eyes, and his fingers trace along the binding. He opens it and gently feels the texture of the paint on paper. Slowly, he closes the cover and for a moment he appears to be asleep

> *The double doors quietly open and Jane is in the doorway, dressed as she was at the beginning. She stands a moment looking all about — at first not seeing Rochester. We, perhaps, might think that we are seeing his dream for a moment but then she quietly moves into the room*

Who is that? What is this?

Jane moves to C

Leah, is that you? (*He does not turn his head, just looks before him*)

Act II, Scene 4

Jane No, sir: it is not.

Jane stands a little behind him. Still he does not turn his head

Rochester Who is it? Who speaks?
Jane Do you not know me, sir?
Rochester Great God — what delusion has come over me? What sweet madness has seized me?

Jane moves and places a hand on his shoulder

Jane No delusion. No madness. It is I, Jane Eyre.
Rochester Jane — Jane! (*He grasps her hand and pulls her round before him*) Is it possible?

They embrace

So often in my dreams you have returned — I dare not hope this is reality.
Jane Do not fear, Edward, this dream will never fade away.
Rochester Can I believe it? Can I trust my senses?
Jane Yes, yes, Edward, I am here. I have come back to you.
Rochester Oh Jane! How — why — why did you come? Is it from pity? Did you hear word of this catastrophe?
Jane I heard not a word until I reached Milcote on my way here. They told me of the fire and of the terrible death, and then some said that you were hurt — caught up in the burning chamber. But when I enquired as to your wounds, no-one did know.
Rochester But you have seen the servants — Mrs Fairfax ... ?
Jane No, no. When I reached this blackened ruin and found the door without attendance, I knew somehow to find you here.
Rochester (*after a slight pause*) Then you do not know?
Jane Know? What is there to know?
Rochester It — it is no matter.
Jane But, sir, if I am not in possession of some vital fact ...
Rochester You have learned all there is to know. Hold me — hold me, Jane.
Jane I do — I will. (*For the first time inspecting his face at close quarters*) What scar is this upon your forehead — was this incurred those nights ago?
Rochester Yes, it was.
Jane And is this the extent of your injuries? What more is there?
Rochester Nothing: nothing more.
Jane Do you speak the truth?
Rochester Of course! I am both fit and well. (*He rises and moves carefully away from her*) But, speak, where have you been these many months — where did you hide yourself? How did you survive?

Jane Sir, there is so much to tell eventually. I found a haven. I am an independent woman now.
Rochester Independent? What do you mean?
Jane I have inherited money. I am my own mistress now.
Rochester Then what brings you here? Why have you returned?
Jane I had to come, Edward. Just four nights ago, near midnight, I was left alone. It was a stormy night and there was a tension in my very bones. Suddenly my heart stopped still for I heard a voice — away — a distant voice, and it cried my name, most distinctly, "Jane", three times it sounded. And there was anguish in the voice and I knew that I must come.
Rochester Then this is God's work indeed, for I did cry. I cried for you, Jane. I asked God if I had not been long enough desolate and might not soon taste bliss and peace once more. And you heard!
Jane (*moving to him*) Oh, sir, I have come back: I will never leave you — I will be your neighbour, your companion. Only say that it is possible, say that you will keep me here.

There is a long pause

Rochester Jane, sweet Jane ... I am unable to keep you here. (*He moves away from her*) You must go back — back from whence you came. You have made another life. Do not destroy it to return here.
Jane But why? What reason is there?
Rochester I have nothing to offer now — my life has changed.
Jane It could never change so much.
Rochester It has, completely.
Jane I do not understand. You have just told me how you longed for me — how you did call for me those nights ago.
Rochester I did call then in anguish but then I was haunted by that being, kept upstairs ...
Jane And now your wife is gone — delivered from her dreadful life.
Rochester Yes ...
Jane And you are free — unchained from all that went before.
Rochester No, Jane; that is not so, for as one manacle fell free, another took its place.
Jane But what — what plagues you now?
Rochester Jane — Jane. (*He comes to her*) I hear your voice: I feel your touch, your presence warms me. I know again the heaven of your embrace, but I cannot see you.
Jane See me ... but sir ...

She stops and stares into his eyes. His gaze is unseeing

Your eyes, Edward, your eyes ...

Act II, Scene 4   65

Rochester It was in the fire: she burnt the very sight from them.
Jane Oh, sir: this grieves me so. Can you not see the very day from night?
Rochester I feel the shadows with the one — the light and dark, nothing more.
Jane Then it is madness that you send me away. I am needed now more than ever I was before. I will be your eyes, your guide, your nurse. I cannot leave you now, and I *will* not.
Rochester Jane, I cannot let this be your life. You must leave.
Jane Never that, sir. I will never leave you and you cannot but accept this.
Rochester No, Jane — no.
Jane I love you, Edward.

Pause

Rochester Oh: and I love you.
Jane Then marry her who loves you: take her unto you for the rest of life.
Rochester Jane, this is not possible.
Jane Everything is possible, Edward. I heard your voice calling for me those many miles away: that was possible. Do you not want me for your wife?
Rochester You know I do — but I am now a blind man ...
Jane What difference does this make?
Rochester I must be led about by the hand ...
Jane Then I take your hand: I'll never let it go.
Rochester I cannot!
Jane Relent, sir, relent!

Pause

Rochester Jane, how can I stem the flow. My heart is rushing out to yours. I cannot let you go — stay, stay, marry me ...
Jane Oh, I will — I will ...
Rochester Then come — come to me at last, little Jane Eyre.

She slowly crosses to him as the music builds and ——

—— the CURTAIN *falls*

FURNITURE AND PROPERTY LIST

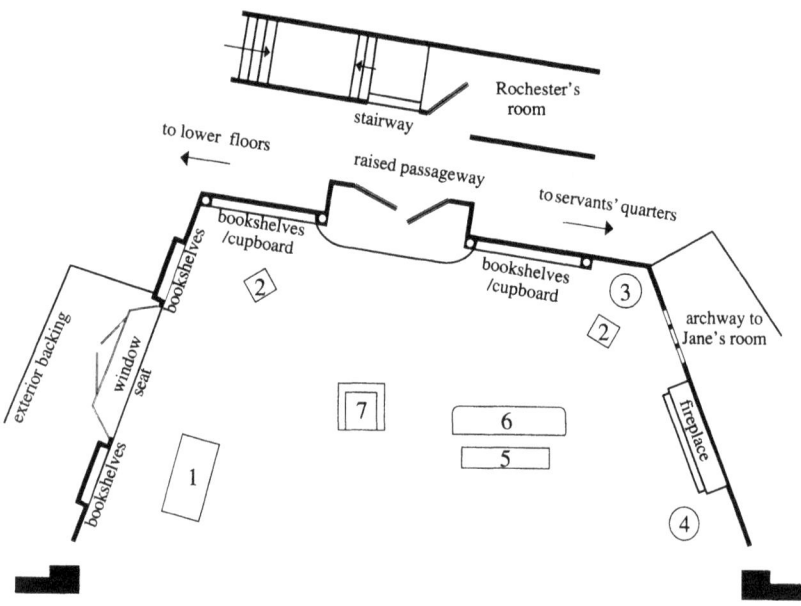

1: table   2: upright chairs   3: pedestal   4: globe   5: long stool   6: settle
7: winged armchair

SETTING NOTE

The library is on the first floor with large double doors entrance from a 6" raised rostrum passageway with a step into the room. In the original production the passageway halls were dressed with tapestries rather than paintings.

The wedding scene is played in front of a single flown stained glass church window, carefully back-lit to darken out the rest of the standing set, and is flown in as Rochester and Jane move to the wedding scene towards the end of Act II, Scene 1 as the wedding music underscores their walk.

After the fire scene (Act II, Scene 3) the bookcase UR should be able to be removed and replaced with a charred double. In the original production the bookcase was built to slide off after the fire to be replaced by a facsimile totally burnt-out and the pillars on either side of the fireplace were turned to show their reverse sides which had been distressed indicating that they had been burnt in the fire.

Jane Eyre 67

ACT I

Scene 1

On stage: Medium-size table
Upright upholstered chairs
Pedestal (optional). *On it*: large bust
Large globe
Long upholstered stool
Period settle
Large winged leather armchair
Recessed bookshelves with cupboards below either side of double doors. *On shelves*: books
Recessed bookshelves either side of window. *On shelves*: books
Fireplace. *Above it*: large portrait of Rochester's father
Small table
Framed maps on walls
Casement window (practical). *Above it*: crucifix. *Either side of it*: curtains (open)
Dressing for passageway walls
Duster for **Leah**

Off stage: Small case, box (**John**)
Tray with bowl of soup and spoon, bread (**Leah**)
Unlighted candle in holder (**Mrs Fairfax**)
Riding crop (**Rochester**)

Scene 2

Re-set: Table in front of window
2 upright chairs at table

Set: Various drawing materials, painting equipment, large portfolio containing several sketches and paintings on table

Off stage: Bags (**John**)
Brandy decanter and glass (**Leah**)

Scene 3

Strike: Decanter of brandy

Off stage: Jug of water (**Jane**)

Scene 4

Set: Cleaning materials for **Leah**
Bottle of brandy in cupboard below bookshelves

Scene 5

Re-set: Curtains closed

Check: Double doors closed

Off stage: Jug of water and towel (**Jane**)
Bandages (**Rochester**)
Phial (**Jane**)

Personal: **Mason**: blood-sac
Jane: smelling salts

ACT II

Scene 1

Re-set: Settle, long footstool, winged armchair away from c
Table DR

Set: Open trunk with straps, clothes c
Jane's box

Check: Double doors and door to **Rochester**'s room open

Off stage: Dress (**Leah**)

Personal: **Rochester**: jewel case
Adèle: posy
Wood: prayer book

Scene 2

Re-set: Settle, long footstool c
Winged armchair upstage of fireplace
Jane's portfolio in cupboard

Set: Small table by winged armchair. *On it*: decanter and glass of brandy

Jane Eyre

Check: Curtains open

Off stage: Jug of water (**John**)
"Burning" brand (**Bertha**)

Scene 4

Strike: Curtains from window
Bookshelves UR
Books from shelves
Upright chairs
Table DR
Globe
Pedestal and bust
Brandy glass and decanter

Re-set: Winged armchair turned towards fireplace with small table beside it
Jane's portfolio in cupboard

Set: Boards across passageway
Charred bookcase UR
Tray of tea on long footstool

Off stage: Small medicine glass (**Mrs Fairfax**)

LIGHTING PLOT

Practical fittings required: candles in library.

Two interiors.

ACT I, Scene 1

To open: General interior lighting, fading daylight effect from window; fireglow

No cues

ACT I, Scene 2

To open: General interior lighting, winter daylight effect from window; fireglow

Cue 1	**Jane** goes into her room	(Page 24)
	Fade to black-out	

ACT I, Scene 3

To open: Black-out

Cue 2	When ready	(Page 24)
	Bring up fireglow and very dim lighting	

ACT I, Scene 4

To open: General interior lighting, daylight effect from window; fireglow

Cue 3	**Rochester** and **Mason** exit	(Page 37)
	Fade to black-out	

ACT I, Scene 5

To open: Fireglow, moonlight through curtains, light in passageway

Cue 4	As scene progresses	(Page 37)
	Change moonlight to sunrise	

Jane Eyre

Cue 5   **Jane** opens the curtains   (Page 41)
Increase lighting in library with sunrise effect from window

ACT II, SCENE 1

To open: General interior lighting, summer daylight effect from window

Cue 6   **Rochester** and **Jane** walk slowly downstage   (Page 49)
Fade to spot downstage

Cue 7   Stained glass window is flown in   (Page 49)
Bring up lighting behind stained glass window

Cue 8   **Wood**: "This is dreadful, quite dreadful!"   (Page 51)
Fade to spot on **Rochester** *and* **Jane**

ACT II, SCENE 2

To open: Night effect from window, general interior lighting, practicals on, fireglow

Cue 9   **Rochester**: "Ooh, Jane ... Jane ... Jane ...   (Page 56)
Fade to black-out

ACT II, SCENE 3

To open: Night effect from window, general interior lighting, practicals on, fireglow

Cue 10   Crash of thunder   (Page 56)
Flash of lightning

Cue 11   Everyone exits   (Page 58)
Flash of lightning

ACT II, SCENE 4

To open: Dismal interior lighting, late afternoon effect from window; fireglow

No cues

EFFECTS PLOT

ACT I

Cue 1	**Mrs Fairfax**: "Go with Leah." *Front doorbell*	(Page 6)
Cue 2	**Jane** stands at the window *Violent gust of wind blows the window open*	(Page 10)
Cue 3	To end SCENE 2 *Music for scene change; fade when ready and fade in sound of wind; doorslam, smoke effect from **Rochester**'s room*	(Page 24)
Cue 4	To end SCENE 4 *Bright music for scene change; fade when ready and fade in sound of wind*	(Page 37)
Cue 5	Hysterical scream *Doorslam*	(Page 38)
Cue 6	**Jane** returns to the window *Horse and carriage retreating*	(Page 41)

ACT II

Cue 7	**Rochester**: "Then take my arm ..." *Softly fade in organ music*	(Page 49)
Cue 8	**Rochester** and **Jane** move into a pool of light *Music rises; fade when ready*	(Page 49)
Cue 9	To open SCENE 3 *Crash of thunder, sound of rain*	(Page 56)
Cue 10	Flash of lightning *Thunder; smoke effect from staircase*	(Page 58)
Cue 11	**Rochester** collapses *Crash of thunder*	(Page 59)
Cue 12	**Rochester**: "... little Jane Eyre." *Music; build to climax*	(Page 65)

www.ingramcontent.com/pod-product-compliance
Ingram Content Group UK Ltd.
Pitfield, Milton Keynes, MK11 3LW, UK
UKHW021845210426
5322IPUK00022B/480